THE POWER IS YOU

RAJESH YADAV

PRABHAT
PRAKASHAN

Published by
PRABHAT PRAKASHAN PVT. LTD.
4/19 Asaf Ali Road,
New Delhi-110002 (INDIA)
e-mail: prabhatbooks@gmail.com

ISBN 978-93-5521-293-1

THE POWER IS 'YOU'
by Rajesh Yadav

Edition
First, 2023

Price
₹ 250 (Rupees Two Hundred Fifty Only)

Printed at
Japan Art, Delhi

Author's Note

This for me is not a mere book. I have aged, learned, tried and even failed, but I never stopped hustling. I live by my life's mantra which is, 'Never Say Never'. This book is an opus of my hard-earned intellect which I whole-heartedly share with each of you. My experiences in life have been a combination of good, bad and everything in between. These twists and turns have taught me a lot in life and through this book I would like to share my earned wisdom of the world along with a few life hacks to simplify the life of the forthcoming generations.

Many have asked me what encouraged you to be a lifecoach? In all sincerity, I was never acquainted with this word 'lifecoach' till recently, when it became an 'in-word'. My path towards my success has been gradual and often toilsome. My passion to walk new paths and take on life's challenges giving it my very best has brought me here. There is no single instance, but a combination of various occurrences and events that have made me who I am today.

My humble beginnings are a constant reminder of how I had to work hard for everything I achieved in life, as nothing was served to me on my plate. Being from a middle class family, I had to take on responsibilities at a very young age. I began to hustle and find innovative ways to make my way through life. I never gave up, nor did I ever give in. There was this fire in me that never diminished and glows brightly even today. It is that fire that made me a national level athlete and made me who I am today.

This is the life most of my Indian brethren face today. Not all of them make it to the top or are able to find ways to succeed. This book is my way of helping the juggernaut part of India's population who are capable of greatness but lack the self-confidence and drive. Through this book, I intend to pave the way for them to reach their full potential.

I acknowledged my inner force in the Almighty, Bhole, who has bestowed me with the gift of life for which I am ever grateful. My parents have been a great source of enlightenment in my life. My wife, my pillar of strength and the light to my world has been with me through thick and thin, trudging through life's journey and sharing in every joy and sorrow. My gurus and teachers have shaped me into the person I am today and continue to be a guiding source in my life.

It is to these people I owe my deepest gratitude. I wish to acknowledge them and devote this book to their support and guidance in my life.

I hope this book helps you find your strengths and overcome your weaknesses to assist you to live life to your full potential.

Happy reading.

Contents

Author's Note 3

PART 1: YOUR MIND IS A POWERHOUSE

1. Cultivating an Attitude of Gratitude 9
2. Think Success from Dreams to Destiny 16
3. More Power to your Will Power 27
4. Facing Challenges with Confidence 36

Thought-Provoking Questions To Ponder On 46

PART 2: ESSENTIAL HABITS FOR SUCCESS

1. High Performance 49
2. Stick to your Ethics 57
3. Why the Need to Manage Time? 64
4. Setting Life Right 71

Thought-Provoking Questions To Ponder On 78

PART 3: KEYS TO BETTER COLLABORATION

1. The Secrets of Communication 81
2. The Relationship Formula 89

3. Be SMART 98

4. Reset your Life 106

Thought-Provoking Questions To Ponder On 113

PART 4: DIRECTING YOUR LIFE'S STORY

1. Who is In-charge? 117

Thought-Provoking Questions To Ponder On 128

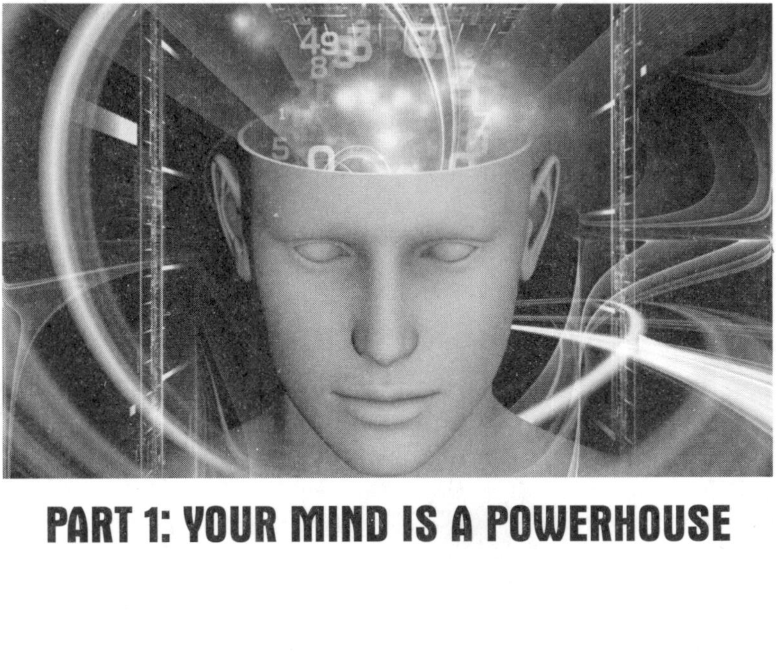

PART 1: YOUR MIND IS A POWERHOUSE

1.
Cultivating an Attitude of Gratitude

"Our life is what our thoughts make it."
— Marcus Aurelius

Are you in control?

There was once a chirpy sales executive who worked in a high-pressure environment. Month after month he struggled to meet his sales targets and so did his teammates. But, never once did his colleagues see him gloomy or depressed. Out of utter curiosity, his team manager asked him how he managed to stay so positive through all this grinding and stress. With his usual twinkle in the eye, he chirpily responded, "It's really simple, I choose to be positive." His confused senior was baffled by this simple answer of 'choice'. He continued to probe, here is his reply:

"Every morning I wake up, I tell myself, 'the choice is mine'. I can choose to be in a good mood or a bad mood today. And I choose 'good' each day. When things go wrong I could choose to feel like a victim or choose to learn from it. I always choose the learning curve. Every time I hear someone complain, I could choose to indulge in their misery or show them a positive outcome. I tend to choose the 'positive side'."

What is attitude then one may ask?

"Attitude is a little thing that makes a big difference."
— Winston S. Churchill

In a nutshell, attitude is nothing but a frame of mind. A picture of how you view yourself, how you decipher others, and the perception you hold of your life's experiences. Your behaviour, your conduct, your moral values, and your social interactions all are crucial parts of your attitude.

Ever heard of the quote, "Your vibe attracts your tribe", which means your energy will attract the exact energy you pour out in the world. Attitude is a very strong attractor, so the more positive your attitude is, the more you can expect positivity to surround you.

This then brings me to the point of the Importance of Attitude:

The difference in people, performance, and outcome all depends on individual attitudes. As I stated earlier, a tiny mental tweak can bring about a colossal change in our outlook towards life. Your attitude is the main ingredient in your recipe for success. The right attitude accompanied by integrity and principles can get you skyrocketing to success in whatever route you choose.

Our attitude can influence our actions. Take this simple example:

Muttiah Muralitharan, a cricketer was asked for his secret behind the highest number of wickets in Test Cricket. His answer was simple: when he bowled his attention was solely on hitting the middle stump. He did not even consider aiming at the left or right stump, merely the centre one. So, every time he bowled the chances of him hitting the middle stump was high and resulted in the highest number of wickets. He currently holds the record for the highest (800) wickets in Test cricket.

Your attitude, not your aptitude,
will determine your altitude.

— Zig Ziglar

So, then the obvious question arises, what are the factors that determine your attitude? Primarily, there are three factors that shape your attitude. Here is a little bit about them:

1. **Surrounding:** Our surroundings have a great effect on how we behave. The right environment can facilitate interactions while a confining one will discourage interactions among people. Similarly, every place that a human spends significant time at will leave a lasting effect on his or her perspective. Let's start at the very beginning, let's begin at home. Our circumstances and atmosphere at home affect how we think, behave, and adjust to life's situations. A happy and settled home will produce a positive outlook on life. A gloomy, detached, and unstable atmosphere in a home can raise a child who has a constantly guarded or a pessimistic perspective. Even at a workplace where a superior is understanding and encouraging, instead of demanding and controlling, will have a lasting positive effect on the attitude of the employees. Our ideas, customs, religious or traditional beliefs and social behaviours that surround us every day in our homes, places of work, friends circle, and more, each becomes a source that drives our attitude. Consider the media we consume, every bit of information we devour influences our feelings and opinions, thus altering our attitudes.

   More the negativity more the attitude of intolerance and of course vice-versa.

   Also, people learn from people. It is innate for humans to mimic the people they revere. Studies show that families and their economic situations have a major influence on the emotions and behaviour of both parents and children. Peers are another set of people who can influence an individual's outlook on life and play a vital role in his or her identity development. Overcritical people questioning one's potential, appearance or intellect can have a negative impact too. Hence, choose your friends wisely; the company you keep ultimately determines who you are.

2. **Situations:** Combined with an environment comes the experience as a packaged deal. Every circumstance, turn of events, or episode we face in our daily life has the insight that accompanies it. We learn from those experiences, some good, some bad, some hanging in between. These insights are what carve our behaviour and govern how we act or react to future situations. As a simple example, a person who has once been cheated on by a lover will most likely have trust issues with his future partners too. He will keep his guard up and avoid wearing his heart on his sleeve. Not everybody who's had their heart broken would necessarily react like that, but you get the gist.

   Every situation is a determining factor and a point of reference to how our attitude is sculpted. The better the experience, the more positive will be the attitude and of course vice-versa.

3. **Schooling:** Here we do not speak of degrees and certifications; rather we dwell on knowledge and wisdom. No matter how well-educated one maybe, his attitude depends on his understanding of people and circumstances. Educational and religious institutions have a huge role to play in laying the foundation of moral concepts and cognizance in an individual. Pedagogy does play a vital role in broadening our horizons, but a lot depends on our value system too. The right set of morals tends to imbibe a sense of compassion and empathy in people. Empathy encourages us to grow profound degrees of affinity and trust with others both at work and in different parts of life. Thus, education in

a broader sense can have a tremendous grip on the behaviour, outlook, and finally the attitude of a person.

You are a metamorphosis of your thoughts, actions, and beliefs.

The Power of Attitude

Attitude is the product of belief; you cannot have an attitude that measures beyond your belief. Ever heard of the elephant rope? When elephants are young, tiny, and docile they are tied by a rope to a post, it keeps them from running away. By this act, they are conditioned to believe that they are bound by the rope. Over the years, this tiny calf grows into a gigantic, majestic creature that possesses enormous strength and can easily break-free from even the toughest clasps. But, by constantly chaining the elephant over the years its trainer has made it submissive. The elephant now believes that it is bound and held by this simple chain, which in all honesty has zero hold over this mammoth of a creature. If only the elephant realizes his power and channelizes it in the right direction, he can attain freedom.

What holds you back?

Yes, it is true we cannot control most circumstances, events, and outcomes in our lives. But, what we can do is focus on the things we have complete control over, that being our Attitude. How we think, act, and react all depends on our perspective. A tiny mental tweak for the better can make a colossal change in our outlook towards life.

When you change the way you look at the world, the world you look at will change. And it all starts with the right attitude. Hence, the pursuit of happiness is a matter of choice. How you view the world around you and what you make of the circumstances that you are involved in each day, is what defines your attitude to life. It is human nature that we tend to undermine our own capabilities to accomplish our goals, while we secretly believe other people possess magical powers to achieve those exact goals.

So, what does it take to develop a positive outlook in life?

1. Focus on what you want, NOT on what you DON'T want.
2. Everything has a reason. Find what that lesson is that every problem teaches you. Memorize it.
3. Not everything you think is true. Sometimes, it's just your mind that is playing up.
4. Express gratitude often.
5. Let go of resistance that is holding you back.
6. Be 100% present in everything you do.
7. Nobody is perfect, accept your imperfection and work with it.
8. Embrace life with all your power.
9. You are in control of your emotions; it should never be vice-versa.
10. Love yourself, because you are MORE THAN ENOUGH.

Most of all believe that you are more than enough.

"Quit searching for essence in everything you've gotten wrong. It's right there in everything you've gotten right. Just get better at it."

— Chinonye J. Chidolue

Be happy

In most scenarios, people link happiness to goals such as security, wealth, and health. Hence they postpone their choice to be happy in the hopes of someday achieving those goals. But the truth is 'Happiness is a choice'. Once you have accepted yourself for who you truly are and have begun to choose the optimistic route at every crossroad, your life will then become a source of inspiration. Surround yourself with the right minds, build relationships with people that motivate and encourage you. You can choose to be happy in the most arduous circumstances, don't wait for a better time or moment. Seize the day before you regret the time you lost.

You have the power to make that change in your life. You have the power to control your reactions and be proactive instead. It is only when you love and embrace yourself will you be truly YOU.

Let your attitude reflect your true character and personality. Shine like a diamond!

"Your attitude will determine your success in life.

If your outlook on life is a positive one, you will find life will be easier. Everything comes down to your own attitude.

And, only you are the one who decides what type of attitude you have, it is your choice!"

— Catherine Pulsifer

❑

2.
Think Success from Dreams to Destiny

"Success depends more on attitude, than on your appearance or talent"

— Rajesh Yadav

What is Success?

There are two kinds of people in life, winners and losers. And guess what, losers get a second chance.

Warren Buffett was once asked how he defined success, this was his response: "If you get to be 65 or 70 and later, and the people that you want to have love you actually do love you, you're a success."

Now that's the definition by one of the most revered and financially successful men in the world. To some success is defined by the money they have accumulated, to another it is finding love. Some consider a life without stress as successful, while for others it is about merely owning a debt free roof over their head.

To a rich man his prosperous business is success, while for a fisherman fishing for his daily meal in the morning while lazing the rest of the day away considers his life a success. To each the definition of success is unique. There cannot be a standard grade system or a benchmark to define success.

Most people do not have a definition of what success means to them. Without a vision, a path or a destination, every move will be trivial and a hindrance leading to a life where one never reaches the desired destination of triumph. To have a goal in mind is a vision, to find a means to reach your goal is the path and when you have achieved that goal you have succeeded.

Success is when reality catches up with your dreams

Some may argue that success in life is not merely about achieving the next immediate goal, but rather finding content in the many facets of life.

What does success mean to you?

Advance in life

"The best investment you can make is in yourself"

— Warren Buffett

Learn to Communicate

Clear communication aids in avoiding misunderstanding and improves your relationships, both personal and official. Effective communication is not merely exchange of information, but rather deciphering the emotions and intentions behind the message. We often tend to mumble indistinctly or incoherently and expect the listener to grasp our thoughts and intent in context. Effective communication requires both clear communication as well as listening skills. To clearly communicate it is vital you choose your words carefully, avoid misleading vocabulary and mixing words.

Never assume the other person may have understood or knows what you mean or what you were talking about.

Take that little effort to clarify and ensure the message you are sending has been received clearly.

Sleep, Eat, Work, Repeat

Don't keep waiting for God to do and luck to arrive, work so hard that neither can move away from your side.

Take care of your body. The daily grind can be tough, but not taking care of your body because of erratic work hours is just an excuse. Set aside some time for exercise each day. Even a 15 minute workout session first thing in the morning, in the comfort of your home will energise you. Put a schedule in place and follow it. Eat well and on time. Ensure your body is not sleep deprived. And most of all, take some 'Me Time' out each week to reflect, slow down and enjoy the true adventure that life is.

You get one body and one life; why not make the most of it?

The right partner

Be it for business or for life, it is essential you pick the right partner. Relationships help determine who you will become. It can drastically heighten your chance of being successful in business as well as in life. Look for that someone who shares the same values as you. One who is supportive of your goals and future plans. Find a partner that is smarter than you, has traits of empathy, respect and is unquestionably trustworthy. A balanced partnership helps bring out the best in both partners, giving each better odds of succeeding in life.

"Great things in business are never done by one person; they're done by a team of people."

— Steve Jobs

Do more than exist – Live!

Are you living a life of intention?

Yes, it is true! What happens in life cannot be controlled, but are you living the life you wanted or are you merely drifting through it? It is like driving on a new path, you are unaware of the condition of the road, its twists or turns. But, you do trust your capability as an excellent and careful driver. Similarly, you are in the driver's seat of your life and have the ability to steer the ride. Your dexterity to deal with challenges that march your way, will determine your direction of the paths you take in life. Choose wisely.

Find that purpose that drives you

"Success is the triumph of the will over imagination"

— Emile Coue

Purpose directs life. When your purpose is clear you are able to differentiate between what you are currently achieving and what you want to truly accomplish. Purpose here doesn't replace goals; they are distinct from each other. If objectives are the interim halts along the way, then purpose is the path to be travelled. When the direction you take in life is meaningful and fulfilling, that's when your life has significance.

Most people are sure of what they do not want in life, people know they do not want to be poor or they do not want to be immoral. But, at the same time they are unaware of what they want in life. The chase after purpose can be sought through self-inquest. Even unforeseen dire external circumstances are another powerful force that drives purpose in people.

For example, Aditi Joshi from Bangalore who is an online crusader set up C-Positive; it is a content platform serving as a lifestyle directive for cancer patients and their caretakers. What triggered this in her? Numerous incidents of cancer in her close knit circle, including her own mother and additionally the staggering statistics that proves cancer is monstrous. There are numerous charities, orphanages, free assistance, awareness campaigns, etc. that are results of such resolute.

Choose your path

What are you efficient at?

Can you envision yourself being successful and prospering in your path of choice?

Will you be devoted to this path for the next 25 years of your life?

Find that area in your life where you have a feeling of competence. Devote time and energy in developing, expanding your skills and talents in that area of competence. This is where you begin to take control of your destiny. Tune out the critics outside and ensure the critic that lies inside you believes too. Be excited about new opportunities in front of you. And above all, do not be ashamed of what you have to do to get there. It all boils down to: What matters to you?

Unless your heart is in the doing, you will not give it your best.

Refuse to give up

Thomas Edison conducted approximately 1,000 failed experiments, but then he invented the light bulb.

The first company Henry Ford started went bankrupt. His second endeavour collapsed as well and he was compelled to leave.

Einstein failed his entrance exam to the Swiss Federal Polytechnic school, he later graduated from college and became an insurance salesman. He quit it because he failed at that as well.

The rest is history.

Failure or even the thought of it can be devastating. When you toil and strive at attaining an objective and it all goes south, it can be frustrating. There are tons of obstacles on the way to success. You must have inner strength and power to overcome it all.

Patience and Consistency

Ever heard of The Chinese Bamboo Tree? This tree comes from a hard nut which is sown. It has to be watered and fertilized every day for 5 years, before it breaks through the ground. During these 5 years of nurturing if there is any hindrance in the watering or fertilization process, the Chinese bamboo tree will cease to survive. But if it survives for five years through the nurturing process and manages to break ground, it can then grow up to 90 feet tall in a matter of just 6 weeks.

The question is does the plant grow 90 feet tall in 5 years or 6 weeks?

5 years is what it took to grow, nurture and build itself strong enough to get to the height it is today. The key is consistency. In today's world of instant gratification we expect results almost immediately. It is hard, but it is worth it. Even when you feel like quitting but your ability to continue the action to give your best is what persistence is. Persistence combined with determination can do wonders.

Signs that you are persistent:

1. You have a goal and are highly motivated to meet it.
2. You are a 100% committed.
3. You have confidence that you will achieve your vision.

4. You are willing to adjust and adapt in any way to achieve success.

5. You constantly are up-skilling yourself to meet perfection.

"Success is not the key to happiness.
Happiness is the key to success. If you love
what you are doing, you will be successful."

— Albert Schweitzer

Shawn Achor, is one of the world's leading experts on the relationship between happiness and success. He proves that if an individual raises his level of happiness and is additionally highly optimistic; he or she is more likely to be successful in any undertaken endeavour. He believes we can rewire ourselves and choose to be happy and optimistic.

Do more than exists – Live.
Do more than touch – Feel.
Do more than look – Observe.
Do more than read – Absorb.
Do more than hear – Listen.
Do more than hear – Understand.

Obstacles

OBSTACLES = OPPORTUNITIES

TO

ACT ON

GROW

PERFORM

PROVE YOURSELF

Story of the birth of a baby Giraffe

When a calf of a giraffe is born it falls 8 feet from its mother's womb on to the ground. What a way to be welcomed to life. And if you think that's excruciating wait till you hear what happens next. While the calf is still dealing with the whole experience of birthing and the 8 foot fall, the mother Giraffe decides to kick the calf. One blow sends the calf tumbling and rolling. Before the calf realizes what just happened the mother gives it another and then another blow. The stunned calf realizes that until it does not quickly stand on its feet and move away the blows will keep coming. So amidst the kicks it tries its best to stand up and run away from the mother's legs. Once the calf does that the mother comes closer to it licking the calf and does not kick it anymore.

You must think, how cruel is a mother giraffe to her off-spring? Well, as cruel as it may sound the mother giraffe is teaching her calf the skills to survive. The tender meat of a calf is devoured by predators like wolves, lions and tigers. The mother giraffe cannot always be around the calf and hence this act of kicking it teaches it to stand up on its own feet and run as fast as it can in times of danger.

In this whole scenario teaches us a very precious life lesson.

Never mind how hard you fall, always remember to pick yourself up and get back on your feet.

The road to success is never a smooth ride, but hard work, passion and perseverance makes the ride worthwhile. There are ought to be snags, struggles and mountains of setbacks. If you can identify these setbacks before they hit you, it gives you the chance to brace for danger and take necessary precautions to curtail the damage. Here are some of the obstacles that you are bound to bump into on your road to success.

1. **Fear:** Fear can be crippling. Fear can be both of failing and of succeeding. It can cripple your courage to dream, your

courage to conquer and your ability to execute. Fear can adversely affect the outcome of your labour. Therefore, it is necessary to recognize your fears, find ways and means to conquer it and finally set on your path to success.

2. **Focus and Planning:** Just as fear is crippling, lack of focus and proper planning can be equally dangerous too. To succeed and achieve any goal, focus is the primary ingredient. Focus is the key to reasoning, solutions, perspectives and decisiveness. Plans are mere blue prints. Unlike a blue print of a concrete structure, business plans can be modified to dynamic situations and ensure you reach your goals. A highly focused individual will be able to yield the best results.

3. **Lack of persistence and goals:** To find success first find your life's goal. What is it you want to do with your life?

   Goal setting is vital for any plan to succeed. Unless you begin with an end in mind, you will never be able to follow a definitive path that meets your objective. As crucial as goal setting is, so is persistence, they go hand-in-hand. Persistence enables you to succeed against all odds. Only if persistence prevails will you reach the point of attaining fulfilment.

   "In the year 2000, when the entire world was celebrating the new century, I was celebrating my disastrous fortune. There were no films, no money, no company, a million legal cases against and the tax authorities had put notice of recovery on my home," Amitabh Bachchan is a fine example of persistence that paid off. He was on the brink of bankruptcy, when he reached out to Yash Chopra and bagged the opportunity to be a part of the cast in *Mohabattein*. From there he began to roll back into the lime-light and soon became the nation's sweetheart through *Kaun Banega Crorepati*. Had it not been for his persistence to try again and his goal to clear his debt, he would have given up, filed for bankruptcy and been just another face in the crowd.

"Persistence is self-discipline in action."

— Brian Tracy

4. **Chaos and Ego:** Ego is like a brick wall. The more you begin to achieve in life, each achievement metamorphoses into a brick of ego. As we continue to prosper our wall of ego keeps getting broader and higher until we cannot reach the people on other side anymore. Ego breeds paranoia, a sense of entitlement and the constant need to control. Before we become selfish and self-centred we should put a stop to our egoism and focus on our abilities to prosper regardless of others.

   Chaos comes in many different forms. These setbacks could be financial, health related, psychological or circumstantial. Insufficient planning or sudden unforeseen expenses could land you into financial chaos. It could cost you your savings, your home or even bankruptcy. Health is another factor. Unforeseen health issues crop up when least expected and can drain you mentally, physically and financially. Sometimes the chaos only exists in our minds or for a short period of time, during which you feel at your wits end. Chaos can be disorienting at times, but in every chaotic situation it is vital that one stays focused, positive and adaptive. Ride the tide, keep moving in the right directions with a positive attitude and let the chaotic situations pass.

"Dreams are connected to the source of your motivation, what is really important for you? What do you dream about?"

— By Marc le Menestrel

To truly be successful in every endeavour one must imbibe in oneself certain qualities that rules over obstacles and guarantees success. Here is the list of qualities to absorb.

Qualities that make you a success:

1. Have faith and confidence that you can achieve anything you put your mind to.
2. Be enthusiastic about making plans, setting goals and achieving them.
3. Set multiple goals, both small and big.
4. Focus on what matters. Fact over fiction, right over wrong.
5. Lead with qualities of self-control, intuition, selflessness and authority.
6. Be disciplined with time, money and habits.
7. Try and create something different. Fail. Then try again.
8. Don't let failure be an obstacle to your success.

Remember:

The secret of success does not merely lie in 'What Men Did', but also in 'What Made Them Do It'.

❑

3.
More Power to your Will Power

A myriad of researches till date have proven that with greater will power comes greater success in life. No matter how well you plan or how much you wish to succeed, without will power none of it is possible. We cannot begin a project without will power and similarly cannot accomplish or succeed without it either.

Our freedom fighter Bhagat Singh went on a hunger strike for over 112+ days to fight against the prejudiced treatment of white prisoners over Indians. Irom Chanu Sharmila, went on a hunger strike on 5th November 2000, for the abolition of Armed Forces (Special Powers) Act, 1958. Finally on 9th August 2016 she ended her fast with a vow to continue to struggle for peace in Manipur. Without determination and willingness these strong men and women would not have been able to take this stance. Their resolute to fight for a cause was backed with a strong will to succeed.

One cannot expect to create a strong will out of thin air or over-night. It takes time, patience and hard work to slowly and steadily expand the boundaries of your will and determination. There are a few proven methods that help you expand the confines of your willingness to persevere.

1. **Switch:** Our body mostly works on auto mode. Eating, drinking, sleeping, working is all done seamlessly without much thought or hindrance. Imagine if you had to do those same tasks with obstacles or certain inadequacies. Consider this; ever since childhood you are a person who has been using your right hand to write. What if for a day you switched hands and began writing with your left hand? How would that make you feel?

   In the beginning it would be amusing and exciting to try something different, but as time passes by you would begin to realise how difficult the task is. Your body and brain are wired to write with your right hand and this change is now a bit confusing, time-consuming and frustrating. Impatience will begin to creep in and you will want to return to writing with your preferred hand. But if you continue with persistence and succeed at completing the task this exercise becomes a means of training your mind and body to fight resistance and willing to accept the change, thus attaining success at your endeavour.

"Luthiel: I cannot change what will happen.
I can only change how I act in the face of it."

— *Robert Fanney*

2. **Chance:** Similar to how you exercise your body for its physical well-being, even the mind does need its share of exercise. At the gym you lift weights to increase your muscle strength and over a period of time you may have gradually gone from 1 to 60 kgs. Precisely like that even your mind needs a chance to exercise its limits and expand its boundaries.

   Today, we are so hooked on to social media that we spend most of our time checking out profiles, statuses and picture of our connections. Whenever we get a break we pick up our phones and scroll through Facebook, Snapchat, Instagram, etc. Sub-consciously we tell ourselves that it is just for a couple of minutes, but the virtual world gets the better of us and we end up spending hours mindlessly scrolling.

Try this simple exercise. Make up your mind that you will avoid being wasteful of your time and will invest it in carefully. So, the next time you have 5 minutes of free time and your hand reaches your phone to unlock it and click on that app, try to stop yourself! Instead of spending time on social media try reading a few pages of an interesting book or doing something that adds value to your knowledge.

3. **Crave:** Often we hear of people with a sweet tooth who habitually have a sweet after lunch and dinner. Chain smokers too are another set of people who crave that next cigarette. Craving is a powerful desire for something. Sometimes these desires are physical things, like those mentioned above, while sometimes they are emotional in nature. The perfect assessment to test ones will power would be to ask them to avoid that one craving they so often desire.

   For example, for a person who is obese due to over-eating the best exercise to test their determination to change themselves would be by giving them a plate of delicacies and asking them not to touch it through the day.

   If you had to take on a similar task, would you fail it or ace it?

"I am, indeed, a king, because I know how to rule myself."

— Pietro Aretino

4. **Meditate:** Meditation is to the mind, as exercise is to the body. It is an easy, non-religious and scientifically proven method of training your mind to reach an emotionally calm and stable state. It teaches you focus and self-control. The art

of meditation helps you cut out the noise, ignore the clutter and see things clearly. Here consistency is key; it is not an easy task to set and follow a routine to regularly meditate. It requires dedication, discipline and the willingness to set aside the worldly pleasures along with the hustle and bustle that daily life offers.

To successfully meditate one must be able to block out all thoughts and merely focus on breathing. It is a difficult task to stop your mind from running wild. Even in quiet and peaceful times your mind tends to wander and jump from one thought to another, most of the times aimlessly. The ability to control your thoughts and concentrate solely on your breathing is how you exert your will power to focus on the task at hand. Meditation is a sure shot way to enhance focus, self-control and discipline.

5. **Purpose:** What is that one reason that gets you out of bed every morning? What adds meaning and satisfaction to your life? If you are still searching for that purpose, follow these few pointers:

   (a) Ask yourself which are your top traits that you stand for? Like happiness, love, togetherness.

   (b) Once you have found your traits how would you best express it to the world around you?

   (c) Delve deep and examine what you enjoy doing the most, where your comfort level is the highest. For example, music could be what you enjoy doing most and you would like to express love or togetherness through what you compose.

   (d) Contemplate on a goal using the above, with a fulfilling end result in mind.

   (e) Persevere to stick to this purpose you have chosen for your life.

"Tis in ourselves that we are thus or thus.
Our bodies are our gardens, to the which our
wills are gardeners.."

— William Shakespeare

When we relate our routine activities to a purpose that brings fulfilment, its only then that we will unearth the will power to succeed.

6. **Target:** Deadlines are a means to moving closer to your goals. But, by merely adding deadlines to all your goals is not going to get you success. There has to be a strategic process to it. When we work towards achieving a goal and have an achievement date in mind the sheer fact of nearing the deadline can have an effect on how we work to achieve it. Some people tend to give up, with the fear that they are not going to complete the task or project in time, while others develop a tunnel vision and are completely focused on meeting the zero hour.

   Deadline keeps us accountable. It can be a catalyst to creativity and innovation even in the most unexpected circumstances. It helps us to understand our priorities better and keeps us in check. Meeting the target date can help raise your confidence and prepare you for success. Setting deadlines is the perfect way to test your will power and empower you.

Think Big

When children enter school, the first thing they are taught is to colour and write. The child is instructed to stay within the boundaries of the drawn figures while colouring. Even while writing, children have to form alphabets within a given set of lines. If they fail to follow these guidelines there are consequences, from scolding to deducting marks for not following instructions.

Over the years in many ways we restrict ourselves from thinking out of the box. There is fear embedded in us that if we try to do something different or unconventional there will be consequences. Hence, we dare not venture 'out of the line'. In the effort to adhere to rules we cripple our creativity, will power and sometimes our future. Our thinking becomes minimalistic, our goals are limited and we act as per our thinking and goals. Consider this, how often do you see a school drop-out succeed in life? Unless, the person is highly motivated, sharp and dedicated to becoming successful the chances are low that he may make it to the top. We need to set our sight high to be able to succeed. As the saying goes:

'Shoot for the moon', even if you
miss you will be among the stars.

We can bank on our will power to help us commit to tasks through effortful control. Will power is a person's innate ability to balance attitudes, thoughts and emotional impulses. A greater will power definitely leads to a better more fulfilled life. It helps you combat stress, deal with hostility and overcome misery. These abilities in turn help you build healthier relationships and a stronger foundation for a bright future.

"If you can't run, you crawl. If you can't crawl—
you find someone to carry you."

— Joss Whedon

What weakens your will power?

Self-Criticism

Here we deal with the idea of how we evaluate ourselves through our own thoughts and ideas. Self- criticism is seen as an individual's negative self-identity. Highly self-critical people tend to have more of a negative outlook on life and are not open to accepting help or support from others. Studies have proven that self-criticism is interconnected to low self-esteem, motivation and poor self-control. In other words if your will power is not strong enough it could lead to acute self-criticism and further develop into depression.

When we feel bad about ourselves we tend to feel guilty and shameful. In a self-critical state we tend to cover those negative feelings by attaining instant pleasure. For example, there are two people who have put on extra weight over the years and have now decided they want to shed those extra pounds. It has been taking them a while to be able to lose that extra weight. Suddenly a single cheat day has been introduced into their diet. Consider one of them is high on self-criticism and the other is not. For the latter, self-compassion plays a vital role and keeps him in check. He will not give into over-indulging even on a cheat day because he understands his goal and wants that positive change, even if it is slow progress. The self-critical one is more likely to over-eat and over-indulge because he feels shameful about his weight and covers it with instant pleasure.

It is vital we all embrace a self-compassionate and a self-improvement mind-set. We should not wait for motivation and encouragement from others. Build a positive and strong relationship within yourself, only then you will be able to build healthier and happier relationships with others.

"Strength does not come from physical capacity.
It comes from an indomitable will."

— Mahatma Gandhi

Temptation

Have you heard about dopamine? When your brain is seeking to reward itself it releases dopamine, which is a neurotransmitter.

When your body is loaded with dopamine it begins to look for instant pleasures, ignoring any long term ramifications that that quick pleasure may carry with it.

A diabetic patient has been avoiding sweet treats for a while now to keep his diabetes in check. After a long week of hard work and completion of an important project, he decides to go out partying to celebrate. At the hotel post dinner, his colleagues order for a variety of dessert. In all the excitement, a bit of cajoling he decided to order dessert too. After all he thought he had earned it. But, that one moment of weakness and temptation may cause him health trouble for days or weeks or may be even months.

Ever noticed, when you visit your grocery store all the exciting foods like biscuits, packed juices, chocolates and other junk food will be at the front or at eye level at the store. These are marketing gimmicks that feed on your reward seeking mode to encourage you to indulge in a few pleasures.

It is important that you realise how you arrive at a specific decision.

Is it your decision or are you working on auto-pilot mode?

Is your will power strong enough to stop you when you begin to drift away?

Think before you act

Will power should not be linked to your ethics or principles. It is a reaction based on your mind and body. This neurological function is a simple reaction to help your body achieve its set goals. Similarly, to exercise will power perfectly we need to add positive goals instead of ones that may have a negative connotation to it. For example, Jasmeet has the habit of drinking tea at least 5 to 8 times a day. She always wanted to give up this habit for better health reasons. She finally makes up her mind from today to avoid it. But the whole day she finds herself distracted and conflicted because she was trying to NOT have her regular tea breaks. The distraction and conflict she experienced hit a negative note within her convincing her to give up the idea of quitting. Only if she had replaced the idea of 'not' or 'don't' with a 'DO', like 'Drink a glass of water every time she felt like having tea'; it would have made the experience easier. The body and mind is more accepting to positive associations rather than negative ones.

What is it that you are going to change and 'do' from today?

Will Power is a skill

Exactly like most of our other skills that we have honed over the years, will power too is a skill we need to hone. Yes, some people are blessed with a stronger will power than you, but that is not a reason to excuse yourself. It is just a matter of time, the sooner you realise and work towards developing your will power, the faster and easier it will get to reach to the goals you have set.

- Avoid negativity that surrounds you.
- Avoid the attitude of pessimism and trust your inner gut feeling.
- Stay away from temptations.
- Instil a strong belief of self-control.
- And above all ... Be happy.

❑

4.
Facing Challenges with Confidence

It is when you face resistance and challenges in what you do, is when you know you are doing something that can make a real change. Keep at it.

'Life is full of challenges.' I'm sure you may have heard this line a million times, especially when you are facing daunting situation in your own life. How we face those challenge says a lot about our outlook in life. We can take every challenge as a severe setback and brood over it till it passes. Or, we can consider it a mere hurdle and do our best to conquer it.

You may have heard the metaphor, 'when life gives you lemons…'. Here, lemons refer to that negative situation or in other words challenges that you face. If you were in a challenging situation and you had to complete that quote, how would you do it?

Anthon St. Maarten, who sounds like an enthusiastic and optimistic human had something like his to say…

When life gives you lemons, you don't just make lemonade. You use the seeds to plant a whole orchard – an entire franchise!

Would your outlook to challenges sound as positive as this one?

Lemons will always be sour, no matter how ripe or raw the fruit is, no one can change its characteristic. It's the other ingredients that are added to it that make the lemon palatable. Similarly, challenges like most bumpy roads, will be troublesome, difficult and demanding; it is your positive or negative attitude towards the situation that will make the ride either effortless or tiring.

What are some of the challenges we face in life?

Fear

Yes, danger is definitely real; you experience it when you encounter life threatening situations. But, fear is nothing but your creative mind running wild. Wise and successful people have a better understanding of fear; they know they have a choice when it comes to fear. Either, they can give in and let fear take control, or they could ignore that sheer feeling and act to overcome it. Most successful people look at facing their fears as an adventure and once they have triumphed over it they feel a sense of pride and true accomplishment.

Perceptions

The day you spend living life to the fullest that is YOUR day, the rest are mere dates in your calendar.

Successful people do not waste their time in caring about what other people think. They do their own thing and make their own way. They believe in being themselves and trusting their gut feelings.

Be who you are and say what you feel,
because those who mind don't matter and
those who matter don't mind.

— Dr. Seuss

If you keep looking for approval, appreciation and acceptance from others, you will live your life for others on their terms and conditions. Yes, we cannot control other people and their reactions to our choices in life, but you can control how you feel and accept their intrusion. Your self-worth should not be measured against another human's achievements. You are unique and cannot measure up to someone else. The criteria's will never match, just like apples and oranges cannot be compared.

Stop caring about opinions of others who do not matter, the ones who truly matter are people who lift your spirits high, accept your imperfections and celebrate your achievements. And they usually do not have opinions and most certainly do not mind.

Negativity

Negative thinking is such a process where we look for the worst in every situation.

One bad interview and you think you'll be jobless forever. One marriage proposal rejected and you believe you are going to be single for the rest of your life. You fell off a bike while learning to ride it and you give up because you believe you will fall off every time you try. These are mental blocks which are brought on by the thought of 'What If?'

Pessimism combined with overthinking can be a terrible combination. A constant sense of negativity and gloominess can lead to depression. Depression though rarely spoken about is real; and if not triumphed over it could lead to suicidal tendencies. Imperfection means failure; sometimes feelings of imperfection may lead to an inferiority complex which is a negative behaviour, brought on by self-criticism or criticism from others. We need to understand the root cause of this negativity, from where it arises, what spurs it and how can it be controlled.

Usually, negativity is self-generated from fear, doubt or ignorance. People with low self-esteem tend to undermine their capabilities, leading to negative thoughts and behaviour. A quote from an ancient scripture defines the human mind as: 'The mind is responsible for both, man's binding and his ultimate liberation, from the cycle of birth-death or happiness-unhappiness. The personality defects in a person are responsible for unhappiness, whereas his qualities are responsible for happiness and contentment.' Our personality defects are the cause of most the negativity that surrounds us. A slight tweak to turn into positive thinkers can make a colossal change in our outlook to life.

To combat pessimism, fear and negative thinking one must have a success driven mind-set. Bringing a positive outlook in life not only can make you successful but can ensure you live a life to you highest potential.

Here are a few pointers to help you overcome negativity, fear and pessimism:

1. Think differently

"Keep your face to the sunshine and you cannot see a shadow."

— Helen Keller

If you want the world around you to change, you need to first bring a change within yourself. Weed out all negative thoughts and behaviours. Try to inculcate a positive expression in every conversation, with yourself and with others. The next time you think of a negative thought like, 'I sucked at the interview; I will definitely not get that job. I don't think I can do this again' Try to change that thought by rephrasing it positively, 'I didn't give this interview my best, but I will work a little harder and try again.' Keep adding positivity to every situation and see how your world changes inside out.

2. Attract positivity

"Once you replace negative thoughts with positive ones, you'll start having positive results."

— Willie Nelson

Change your energy and the world around will change how it reacts to you. Change can be terrifying, but one step towards change and it can do wonders. Once you have inculcated a positive outlook in everything you encounter in life that's when you begin to naturally attract positive people too. Here you must take the initiative to separate yourself from people who are pessimistic and have a negative approach to life. Surround yourself with positive thinkers who encourage you and aid your growth story. Turning yourself from a pessimist to an optimist is a slow process, the best way is to have your friends and family aid you through encouragement and appreciation.

3. Attitude of gratitude

Being self-centred and selfish will get you nowhere. We humans tend to think more about ourselves and what we need from every situation. Be it in conversations with others, when at work, when at play, we put our desire before others. In the process of selfishness we begin to live a life of expectations and become needy. Every situation we weigh it on the intention of receiving and end up sour or unhappy if we fail to receive. The constant need for receiving leaves us unfulfilled and unhappy which later turns into negativity, fear and pessimism.

Lay low on expectations. Do not look at every situation keeping 'YOU' at the centre, try to walk in the others shoe and see the world from their eyes. Help others, accept them and be grateful for whatever they have to offer you in life. This attitude of gratitude is infectious. People will begin to see the positive, giving attitude in all that you do. You will gain more fruitful relationships, which will bring about happiness and positivity in you.

4. Be Responsible

"Take charge of your life! The tides do not command the ship. The sailor does."

— Ogwo David Emenike

You are in charge of your life, you hold the reins. We all get one life; it is our duty to ensure we make the most of it to the best of our ability. When difficulties arise or when we make mistakes we always look for a reason to blame it on.

I didn't get to work on time because I missed my bus.

Ok. But the question is, how often do you miss the bus? Is it a once-in-a-blue-moon occurrence or is it a weekly one? What are you going to do to ensure you do not miss the bus the next week and the weeks after that? Just like this situation we look for reasons to excuse our behaviour in every situation. We do not like to admit to failure. This 'I am always right' attitude does not do harm to anyone else but to ourselves. Remember, you hold the reins. You have the choice and ability to tweak a change and make a difference. You have the choice to wake up earlier and catch the earlier bus instead. Will you do it?

Take charge, take responsibility. Get over the victim mentality and move towards 'I will make a change' thought process. When you change the way you look at situations, that is from a 'I am in charge' perspective you will notice that no one can make you feel inferior, incompetent or unaccepted. These circumstantial apprehensions are merely our own perceptions and that will change into positives once we make that tweak and take control, take charge and be responsible.

I Am Possible

I M POSSIBLE

Once you have dealt with fear, negativity and pessimism you will realise there are no challenges in life that are impossible. An optimistic you have so much more to give to life.

Let it not end there.

Now that you realise that challenges from life and others have no hold on you, its time you challenged life. Your true inner being will reveal itself in difficult times. Take up a new outlook to life, challenge yourself to better yourself. Test your limits, move out of your comfort zone and see how far can you stretch?

Successful people thrive on challenges. Pushing boundaries lets them raise the bar and aim for higher of success. It helps them become more buoyant and increases their self-confidence.

How can you raise the bar and challenge yourself for a better life ahead?

1. **Read:** Challenge yourself to become a voracious reader. Put a figure to a minimum number of pages to be read each day. Pick content that will help you bring a change the negative areas of your life. Reading not only improves your memory but also helps in building a positive attitude, reduces depression and helps raise your level of empathy towards others. Some of your voracious readers are Albert Einstein, Warren Buffet, Bill Gates, Jeff Bezos and Malala Yousafzai, all successful leaders in their domain.

2. **Strengthen:** Take on a routine of tough exercises and follow it to the T. Choose a body type you may not have believed you could ever have and work towards gaining it. Make a change to overcome a lethargic attitude on the weekends. Set a deadline to wake up early even on weekends and begin your day early. Set a diet in place and follow it strictly, and if you can avoid cheat days too.

3. **Give:** Set a goal to help one needy person each week. It may be helping a weak kid in his studies or a jobless person prepare for an interview. This attitude of giving helps you enhance your empathy, it brings about a sense of social awareness and makes you aware of your role to help others in life. The more you give the more you get in return.

4. **Restrain:** Restrain from bad habits and negative influences. Set a target to not gossip about another for a period of 30 days. Or, if you are a chain smoker, give up smoking for a month. Set a time limit for scrolling through your social media accounts. Avoid binge watching your favourite shows online.

5. **Learn:** Beside the knowledge you gain from reading make it a habit to learn something new each day. Be it a set of new words, honing a new skill over the next 2 weeks, learning to drive or ride, etc. Pick a task of your choice, something that you may have wanted to do for a while and accomplishing which will give you a sense of true success.

Facing challenges

Congratulations! You have proven to yourself that you can do anything if you put your heart and mind to it.

The next step is to face any challenge head-on. All it takes are these few steps to ensure you are equipped to face every challenge bravely.

1. **Face it:**

The life of a butterfly begins with a struggle to push its body out of the tiny hole of its cocoon. If it does not go through that struggle it will not strengthen its beautiful wings.

Remember, running away is never an option. Sometimes you feel like the next big challenge is too tormenting and difficult to manage. By sweeping it under the carpet or avoiding it today does not mean the challenge will disappear. Put on your brave face and look it square in the eye. In most circumstance once we have overcome that daunting challenge which once looked humongous to us, we realise that it wasn't that big of a deal after all. Every hurdle you meet will be difficult at first, but practice and persistence will help you cross every hurdle, big or small.

2. **You believe:** You are what you think you are. If you believe you are weak, unworthy or incapable then that is the way you will feel when you are faced with challenges too. Your mind is a powerhouse, you have the potential, you are strong and resilient. With a belief like this, you will already have every tool you need to burn down competition, break the glass ceiling, make that presentation or crack that interview. It merely takes belief. Believe and trust your own potential.

3. **Self-assess:** Depending on others for help once in a while is Ok. But, don't depend on others to get you out every

sticky situation. Depending on others for their opinions, suggestions and solutions is a waste of time. All that people can do is suggest a solution, but you are the best judge of your situation. No one will gain the insight you have until they walk in your shoes. Take a call based on your assessment of the obstacle you are facing, your capabilities and assets. The more time you waste taking opinions from others the more complicated the situation will get.

4. **Emotional check:** When faced with difficulties, one must never try to overcome it with an emotional mind-set. An overwhelmed mind will never give you the best output. Learn to draw a line between practicality and emotions. The perfect balance of the two is excellent, but as soon as emotions get the better of you practicality gets flung out the window. The best way to separate your emotions would be by unlinking your mind to the after effects, the dread or the fear of failure. Focus on the task at hand and try your best to not overthink the final result. Disengaging yourself from consequences is the best way to stay practical.

❑

Thought-Provoking Questions To Ponder On

- What holds you back?
- What does success mean to you?
- What are you efficient at?
- Can you envision yourself being successful and prospering in your path of choice?
- Will you be devoted to this path for the next 25 years of your life?
- What weakens your will power?
- Is it your decision or are you working on auto- pilot mode?
- Is your will power strong enough to stop you when you begin to drift away?
- How can you raise the bar and challenge yourself for a better life ahead?

PART 2: ESSENTIAL HABITS FOR SUCCESS

1.
High Performance

The formula for success lies in doing what an average person will refrain from doing.

— Rajesh Yadav

There are two kinds of people; one who sets goals, the other that chooses not to. People who lack the desire to set goals are unlikely to be successful in life as compared to those that have definitive milestones to reach. Individuals that set goals and even write them down are more likely to accomplish those set goals.

Goal setting

A goal is a futuristic state of being that a person plans to achieve as a desire to an end-point. They are a set of curated milestones that are designed to ultimately lead us to a happier fulfilled life. It gives us momentum and courage to stand against adversities that come in the way of our achievements. In other words, goals are dreams, but with a deadline attributed to it.

Many articles written in the past by leading news publishing sites quote a '*Goal Setting Study*' done by either Harvard or Yale stating, '*3% of Harvard MBAs make ten times as much as the other 97% combined.*' Unfortunately, this study never did take place in reality. Nevertheless, there is much evidence to prove that a written set of goals is truly effective. How?

Commitment

The task of jotting down your goals is a conscious effort that proves you are motivated to make a change in your current situation. This stands to prove you are committed to a transformation and you are now determined to achieve what you have set your sight on.

A commitment to change is the first step in goal setting. Commitment refers to how profoundly dedicated a person is to accomplish set goals, no matter what obstacles come his/her way. Establishing goals with a lack of dedication to achieving it is senseless.

Commitment is the glue that bonds you to your goals.
— Jill Koenig

Accountability

You may have great ambitions and the ability to achieve it seamlessly, but without a roadmap and the will power, the route can get complicated. A written statement of your goals creates a sense of accountability. It takes immense effort and dedication to continue to stay accountable. The path to success is not easy, the routes can often be difficult, unimaginable, and ever-changing. Your fluidity to adapt yourself all while remaining committed to achieving what you have set out for proves your level of accountability.

Do you have what it takes to stay accountable to your goals?

Why is goal setting so important?

Pinpoint a successful person; preferably a rags to riches story. It could be a star celebrity, an accomplished businessman, a super chef, or your successful batch mate. Analyze that person's life and see how he/she was able to turnaround the circumstances and emerge a winner. In all cases, you are bound to find discipline at the core. Discipline in life is essential to success. While for some people it is innate, for others it may take days, months, or even years of practice to stay disciplined. Setting goals requires long-term planning and immense amounts of motivation. To stick to your plan and constantly be motivated one must be disciplined and stay the course. This will help you focus on your ambition, organize your resources to the best of your ability, and be determined no matter what to ensure you achieve your set goal.

"All who have accomplished great things have had a great aim, have fixed their gaze on a goal which was high, one which sometimes seemed impossible."

— Orison Swett Marden

Self-actualization

Staying within your comfort zone has never got anybody anywhere. Life will become boring and predictable; and so will your results. To attain different results you must have thoughts and goals that motivate change. Change comes only when a person truly moves beyond his/her comfort zone. To do that you need to know yourself thoroughly; this includes the question of what you are capable of? The realization of understanding one's own fullest potential and seeking inner growth is where self-actualization begins. Seeking a 'better you' and becoming the best version of yourself requires you to understand:

Who you are?
What would you love to become?
How much you want to earn?
What do you want to own?
Where you'd want to live?

And so on…

It is the motivation one feels towards beginning personal development. Through a better understanding of yourself and the potential hidden in you, you become capable of maximizing your internal growth. You reflect on what you currently are and where you want to be in the future, which are in fact answers to the questions above. This is the path to self-actualization.

The question that can stir up this conversation within yourself is, "What do you really want?" Start by finding a goal that resonates with what you want.

I want to be rich.
I want to be successful.
I want to be powerful.

What is it that will truly bring you happiness? If being successful is your goal, then start by defining what success means to you? How do you believe you can attain it? What do you need, to be successful? The answers to these questions are like milestones that you set for yourself on the path to success. Through self-actualization, you become aware of your potential and ability to attain the success you have planned for.

Choose goals that are truly aligned with your happiness.

We set goals in all enthusiasm at the beginning of each year. Our 'new idea' for the 'new us' is made in the hope of turning our lives around. Unfortunately, with our set habits, crazy routines, and a cozy comfort zone fade our hope for a change. So why do our goals fall through? The problem most of us face while setting goals is that we do not structure it properly. Our goals are vague and lack relevance.

Take for instance Amit, he has this yearning deep down that he wants to '*to be successful*'. Amit does not know how he is going to be successful, or what he is going to do to be successful. He lacks a plan, a roadmap, and milestones to map his journey towards success. Despite the fact that Amit works hard at his career, at savings and investing, yet he finds it difficult to achieve his idea of success because of his scattered view at it. Some days he sees success in career, another day in investing, and so on. What he is missing is a structured approach towards one direction.

Goals cannot be castles in the air. They have to be relevant to you. *A student cannot set a goal to be a doctor if he is inclined towards a career in art.*

Let's take a look at how we can be smart and streamlined in setting goals that are relevant, achievable, and measurable.

GOALS MUST BE SMART

Well-defined

Goals that are vague in nature are the ones that remain unachieved. Generalized goals like 'I will lose weight and become healthier this year', which is one of the most common goals set by people at the beginning of each year fail. It fails because it is not specific.

How much weight do you want to lose?
What do you mean by healthier?

Be more specific. Set a target to that goal to make it attainable. Choose the ideal weight you want to be and make that target weight your goal. Make a monthly, biweekly, weekly, or even a daily target of how much calories you have to burn to reach your ideal weight as per your set deadline.

"In the absence of clearly-defined goals, we become strangely loyal to performing daily trivia until ultimately we become enslaved by it."

— Robert A. Heinlein

Milestones

Milestones are a way of ensuring that you remain on track and do not steer away. Every milestone crossed tells you how much closer you are to achieving what you have set out to. It gives you a sense of accomplishment. Milestones work well for goals that are hard to achieve, breaking down an enormous task into smaller achievable tasks makes reaching your target easier. A sense of achievement in smaller targets helps boosts your spirits and motivates you to stay on track to achieve your goal.

If writing a 300 page novel is your goal, avoid thinking of it as a complete task of 300 pages. When thought of as a whole, the task becomes daunting and tedious and you are bound to give it up. Break that task into chapters, pages, or even words if need be. Choose to write 100 words in the next hour. Suddenly, 100 words don't seem so difficult or unattainable anymore. If you work 8 hours a day, set a routine of writing 100 words every consecutive hour in a day. By the end of day 1, you would have completed over 400 words. A task of 300 pages when broken down to simpler achievable milestones, become simple and doable.

Direction

We often get lost and possibly carried away in the process of setting goals. We tend to lose sight of what we truly want and end up chasing milestones that are irrelevant to us.

Tina is a graduate working for a renowned organization and sees the need to be an MBA to be promoted to the managerial level. Tina's goal is to become a manager in the next two years. Tina's friend has joined a course to learn fluent German and narrates to Tina how interesting the language is. Tina decides she wants to pursue a German course as well and ends up spending 2 hours a day post her office timings to attend the course. A couple of months down the line Tina becomes fluent in German, but then what? Does she want to relocate to Germany? No!

Her time spent in learning a new language is a waste if she does not plan to use it in the future. She could have rather used those hours to study for her MBA that would align with her goal to be a manager. Choosing milestones that guide you in the direction of your goal is vital. One should avoid distractions that come along the way, cut the noise, and follow the plan to accomplish what you set out to achieve.

Deadlines

Above all the others what's important is to set a time limit or an expiry date for your goals. Without a deadline achieving your milestones will be an on-going process and you will never reach your destination.

Avoid having a single deadline to achieve, add deadlines to deadlines.

For instance, Jacob wants to accumulate an emergency fund or ₹ 6,00,000 before the end of the year. This buffer fund will ensure his family's basic expenses are taken care of for a minimum of 6 months in case he loses his job in any unforeseen circumstance. His current income and expenses allow him to save ₹ 30,000 a month. He needs to find ways to save the extra ₹ 20,000 each month. He works out a plan where he can put in an additional 5 hours of work each weekend as a freelancer and earn 20k for it. He follows the plan and ensures the additional 5 hours of deadlines each week are clocked in. This extra effort makes him his extra bucks helping him attain his goal for ₹ 6,00,000 by the end of the year.

"...deadlines get jobs done :)"

— Cahit Kargi

Habits

Make it a habit to write down your goals and review them on an on-going basis. Tweak it from time to time to align them with your ideal future. Ensure your other habits do not come in the way of you achieving your smaller milestones. Follow a pattern of behaviour that brings out the best in you. Avoid habits that lead to addictions. Find ways to energize your body and keep your mind occupied and happy at all times for high performance. A clear mind can work wonders.

Our circumstances change and so also do our thoughts and plans of the future and what we want to achieve. Goal setting is not a one-time activity. It requires continuous evaluation. Re-visiting your goals on a periodical basis will ensure your goals stay relevant and attainable.

And lastly...

"Don't lower your expectations to meet your performance. Raise your level of performance to meet your expectations."

— Ralph Marston

❑

2.
Stick to your Ethics

Choose goals that are truly aligned with your happiness.

A 35-year-old highly educated and ethical financial officer was once offered a rare opportunity to turn around his fortune. Accepting the offer would mean he would be able to afford early retirement with a financially secured life ahead. But this would come at a cost; the opportunity meant helping a bunch of affluent individuals launder their black money. Obviously this would be an unlawful act but he was offered complete security in case he ever got caught. He had to make a decision between financial freedom and moral ethics.

He consulted his wife to know what she would have done if she had such an offer. This is what she had to say, "Every day when I wake up in the morning I watch you sound asleep like a baby. This good night's rest that you enjoy is not because of your financial status, but because of your morals and ethics. Deep down you know you have not wronged anyone and have done the best you can in life. If you accept this offer, will you be able to continue to have a good night's rest?" He knew what he had to do next.

Ethics may be a small word, but weighs a ton in meaning. It encompasses morals, justice, trust, concern, faith, principles, ideals, and much more. It is about making the right choices based on a humanitarian and social outlook. Choosing right over wrong, justice over crime, and virtue over vices is what should govern humanity. Ethics is the basis of every religion and should be the basis of humanity.

Have you ever realized how animals behave selfishly, acting on their desires of hunger and greed? Take hunting for instance; a lion would die of hunger if hunting was against his moral ethics. We humans on the other hand have the ability to care for the other. The fact that we live in a society and follow its inferred norms in many ways governs the way we act and react. Unfortunately, we also are a part of the animal kingdom and have to constantly battle our selfish desires. Suppressing these desires means living within the norms of society. Some struggle and fail to control their desires and end up becoming outcasts.

Unethical living would result in a total malfunction in the way society functions. Our awareness towards a life of morality ensures we understand the difference between right and wrong, good and bad, etc. Our choice to pick honesty over lies or love over hate is our way of ethical living that is guided by our set of morals. In the earlier example of the 35-year-old financial officer, his morals of knowing the difference between right and wrong guided him to make the right decision of rejecting the offer of boat loads of money for doing something dishonest.

Have you come across a situation where you had to choose between your desire and ethics? What did you choose?

"A man without ethics is a wild beast loosed upon the world"

— Albert Camus

Your ethics come into play when you face these questions in life:

1. How can a good life be lived?
2. What are my rights and obligations to be human being?
3. Who decides what is right and wrong or good and bad?

The human concept of ethics is derived from the deep-rooted combination of religion, philosophies, and cultures. Discussion on what is wrong or right is often taken into consideration based on religious or philosophical teachings or even cultural attitudes of the past. To site a relatable example, in certain religious cultures in India eating meat is considered a wrongdoing, while in another culture renunciation of all worldly pleasures or passions is considered a path to enlightenment.

"Never let your sense of morals get in the way of doing what's right."

— Isaac Asimov

Personal Ethics

The context of Asimov's quote above refers to morals being subjective. Each individual has his own ideologies that he adheres to. These concepts are formed based on our experiences at home, in our communities, and in our lives at large. Our religious and political inclinations form biases which additionally mould how we act and behave.

Let us take the example of a man sitting in his car while a child comes begging for money. The man refuses to give the child money and rather offers to buy the child a sandwich. The child refuses the sandwich and keeps demanding for money. The man abstains from giving the child any money and sticks to his offer for food instead. Here the man acted based on his knowledge of how street children are often misguided or forced by their adults into begging for easy money. According to him, this is unethical and by giving the child money he will be encouraging him to continue his begging spree. His ethics discourage him from being a part of this hideous act. Yet his morals has encouraged him to help this child and hence he had offered a sandwich instead.

According to you, was the man wrong in his reluctance to hand over money to the child?

Right and wrong, good and bad can be subjective based on our individual thoughts, understanding, and experiences. There is no universal rule book on ethics and morals that can guide us through life. You may choose a religion or a way of life that suits your ideologies, while your closets friend may not subscribe to the same. But, that does not mean you cannot be friends because your ideologies do not resonate, does it?

Our personal choices must be guided based on a strong foundation of morality. This way we can ensure we make the right decisions in life that we will not have to regret later. It all begins at home. The choice a child makes when his mom gives him a jar of cookies and leaves the room saying, "Take just one cookie and put the jar away. I trust you." The child's choice in obeying or disobeying his mother's instructions will prove his ethical upbringing.

As adults, we do not realize how our children watch and record our actions and imply it. Take the example of a kid pretending to be her dad working on the phone. Her act is a copy of her dad chatting away busily on the phone while she paces the room to and fro. Suddenly, the child starts yelling and ends her make-belief conversation with a bad word, something she may have seen her father do. Hearing this she gets schooled by her parents for using a bad word. She is now obviously confused, in her opinion she didn't do anything wrong, she just did what daddy did!

It can be funny at times when we each look at a situation through our life's eyeglasses and interpret what we see based on our beliefs and understanding. It is like the seven blind men who touched different parts of the same elephant and came up with different ideas and understanding of what an elephant is. Personal ethics falls in a similar thought process and cannot be constrained to a single line of thought. What is important is that in every action we ensure not to harm another to satisfy our own selfish desires.

"Integrity has no need of rules."

— Albert Camus

Business Ethics

The standard of ethics in business is not too far off from the ethical standards in our personal lives. The same rule applies, which is 'there are no rules in ethics'. In business, the actions and decisions taken by people in an organization must watch over and guide the line of business and its functionalities. They need to ensure that in no way their business crosses society's norms and legal boundaries. This includes governing the behaviour of those employed in the line of business as well, in other words 'employee conduct'.

So, the question then arises,

Why is it then that businesses go corrupt or employees get sacked for unethical behaviour?

Here are some of the reasons I could think of:

Profit over Ethics

The sole purpose of a business is to earn profits. Unfortunately, the more money we get the more we want. A profitable business tends to get business leaders eager to find faster ways to grow their business and profitability. This greed may lead them to take calls that could be unethical in nature.

For instance, a manufacturing plant is capable of an output of 10,000 units of a product a day and gives the business overall profitability of 25%. The CEO of the organization realizes the demand for his product is way higher than supply, which if ramped up could earn him a profitability of 40%. He instructs his employees to speed-up the pace of production. Employees confide in him, letting him know that they are already doing their best, a further speed-up would mean a drastic fall in the quality of the final product. The CEO continues to push for higher volume output even if it meant low-quality so that he could reach his goal of 40% profitability.

As humans, our selfish attitude could often lead to our downfall. A business carried out with a selfish vested interest or greed by putting its customers at a disadvantage falls under an unethical tag.

Perform or Quit

Another reason for lack of ethics in business is pressure. When employees are under tremendous pressure to perform they seek measures beyond their moral standards. An employee with a family of 3 dependants would do anything to hold onto his job which pays the bills and feeds his family.

Lack of money, mounting bills, and not so promising future can encourage a person to risk his morality and turn to dishonesty. It is not that the person is dishonest it is the circumstance that leads him down that path. A salesman miss-selling a product to meet his sales target; a doctor ordering unnecessary medical tests for his cut; a student bribing a teacher for better marks, all these are signs of unethical behaviour due to mounting pressure to perform.

"Your reputation is more important than your pay check, and your integrity is worth more than your career."

— ***Ryan Freitas***

Ethics and success go hand-in-hand

The principle of ethics guides us to decipher what is right and wrong. Living a completely ethical life is most likely a myth, but it is simultaneously not impossible. As difficult as that may sound the basis of morality is to put the other first. A husband (and father) loves his family and puts their needs and desires before his. He works hard towards ensuring they get all they need, a roof over their head, food in the belly, the right education and more. It is morally impossible for him to overlook them for his personal selfish needs. Similarly so, if every human would be more mindful of their behaviour and how it affects the other, their empathy towards the other would make it impossible for them to do anything that goes beyond their moral compass.

"Try to find the path of least resistance and use it without harming others. Live with integrity and morality, not only with people but with all beings."

— Steven Seagal

Our moral compass guides us through life and the curve balls it throws at us. As every action has an equal reaction, so also every choice we make in life has a consequence. These consequences will have its effects on us and our near and dear ones. It is up to us to decipher whether we are willing to take on responsibility for the consequences our actions bring.

There is no right answer to the ethical choices we make. The reason we have morals to guide us in life ensures we live a full and happy life, knowing that we did the right thing when we were put on the spot. This is all one needs to be able to gain that restful sleep at night.

Do you sleep like a baby every night?

❑

3.
Why the Need to Manage Time?

"In the past, we looked for future opportunities
and in the present we reminiscence the past"
— Rajesh Yadav

Time and tide wait for no man. OR Time is money; these are such common lines; every human being across the globe would have heard at some point in their lives. But, how many of us have truly understood the value of time? Not many, unfortunately! For those who do value time may have possibly learned its value the hard way.

Do you value your time?
The value of time

Ask the student who failed in his final exams, what is the value of a year.

Ask the mother who gave birth to a newborn for the value of every month.

Ask a shopkeeper who toils daily without a weekly off for the value of a week.

Ask a daily wage worker how valuable a day is.

Ask a traveller who missed his flight for the value of an hour.

Ask a lover the value of every minute while he waits for the love of his life to arrive.

Ask a person who got saved from an accident for the value of a second.

Ask an Olympian who won the gold for the value of a split second.

Time Management

"The bad news is time flies. The good news is you're the pilot"

— Michael Altshuler

Time is a precious gift. Each day when we wake up we are gifted with 24 hours. This gift comes with no expectations, no boundaries, and no questions. You are free to do as you please with your time each day.

How you account for every precious minute each day will define how successful you will be in life. This does not mean one must become a slave to time by scheduling every moment to eat, sleep, work, pray, etc. each day. You have the freedom to choose how you want to spend your time, in ways that are important to you, and help you grow. Put your priorities in place at the beginning each day. Create a to-do list, this helps you prioritize as well as remember your tasks at hand. Make a time table that suits your daily schedule and try to stick to it. Although, do not let the schedule rule your life, remember you are in charge.

I don't have time.

"The next time you hear a person say,
'I don't have time' or 'I have no time,'
Take a moment to be with them.
Without time, that somebody becomes a nobody."

— J.R. Rim

If you are someone who loses track of time easily, set reminders for each important task and these don't need to be just for work activities, it could be for exercises, a walk or even a simple reminder to drink a glass of water every hour. These small initiatives will help you value time better.

Setting specific time slots for every activity will make you realize you have enough time each day to complete your tasks at hand and still have more - for yourself. Another vital point, schedule some 'Me Time' each day, even if it is as little as 15 minutes. Take a break, meditate, dance, sing or simply sit and relax. Ensure this time is not invaded by phone calls or texting or scrolling through social media. Once you begin to schedule your day, you will realize that *'I don't have time'* was just a misconception that you believed in.

Prioritize

"It is not a daily increase, but a daily decrease.
Hack away at the inessentials."

— Bruce Lee

Having a to-do-list is a simple activity that must be done at the beginning of each day. It simplifies your day and helps you keep track of the things you do. How does one prioritize? Start by roughly listing your activities for the day. Then sort those activities into 3 parts.

The first part will be tasks that require your immediate attention, like preparing for a presentation you have to give that day or acting on projects which have deadlines.

The second part of your activities will include tasks that are important but do not need your immediate attention; like paying a bill due by the end of the day, exercising, or wishing a friend for his/her birthday.

The third and last part of your list will have tasks that are neither important nor have a deadline such as reading a book or writing a blog. This does not mean that the third set of tasks can be skipped, they are equally important but not as important as part one and two.

Prioritizing has its benefits. It helps you make the best use of your time and focus well on your activities each day. It assists in the completion of tasks on time and avoids deviation. Above all it helps you plan ahead of time, ensuring you make the most of each minute of every day.

Mindless activities

"Lack of direction, not lack of time, is the problem. We all have twenty-four hours a day."

— Zig Ziglar

Have you ever spent a lazy weekend in bed most of the morning, woken up directly for lunch and spent the afternoon binge-watching your favourite series only to realize later and feel guilty about wasting the entire 48 hours of your weekend? Well! We all have done that at some point in our lives. The important part is realizing the value of that wasted time and not repeating it (too often).

Today's tech-savvy generation is so hooked to their phones that they do not realize the amount of time is spent in mindlessly scrolling through social media. Similarly, we all do tasks each day that do not need our complete attention. *How can we turn these mindless activities into valuable ones?*

Take your commute to work each day as an example, say you spend 2 hours traveling where you are either walking to work or sitting in your transport. This is the time we usually spend scrolling through our phones or chatting with someone. Can we choose to spend those two hours each day learning a new skill or a language instead? All it would take is some time in loading the right audio, video on a device, or carrying a book. You will realize those two hours each day are a powerful time to work on your dreams or goals or desires that you otherwise thought you lacked the time to fulfill. Make every moment count; use it to the best of your ability.

Focus

Time = life; therefore, waste your time and waste of your life, or master your time and master your life.

— Alan Lakein

Usain Bolt, a Jamaican sprinter holds multiple records and dominates the world's toughest sprint competition. He is regarded as the best sprinter across the globe. His performance in the past Olympics of 2008 and 2012 have been par excellence.

His races took barely minutes to complete winning him multiple gold medals. While what we saw was a couple of minutes of his marvellous sprinting, he spent years preparing for it. He spends endless hours in practice day and night, in the culmination of which he reaps its benefits today. His focus on his goal was strong. In spite of his Olympic win in 2008, he immediately got back to practicing for the next race without wasting time in extra-long holidaying, celebrations, or time-out. His dedication to his sport has made him what he is today.

Focus is a vital ingredient in success. If you do not focus your time, strength and attention on your goals you will keep drifting away mindlessly into activities that waste your time and add zero value to your life. To keep yourself focussed you need to create an atmosphere around you that works as a reminder of your goals.

Create a goal board where you write down or can picture your ultimate goals come to life. Revisit these goals often; possibly every week, reminding you to stay on track to what is essential in your life. Make time to re-evaluate your goals periodically; we humans evolve with time and so do our priorities. What we planned for tomorrow could change in the very next minute.

Ordinary people think of how they can spend their time. Successful people think of how they can invest it.

What are the benefits when you manage your time effectively?

- Your days will be more fruitful, you will be able to get more things done and achieve better productivity.
- Your workload will be more manageable and deadlines will be less stressful.
- Better time management will ensure there is less friction in life, no more forgotten meetings, deadlines, or tasks.
- Focus will help you increase your efficiency levels.
- Increased efficiency will reduce re-works that you may have spent time on previously, freeing up your time to do more.
- Better efficiency and time management increase reliability, making you someone trustworthy to do the job well and in-time.
- More time will translate into more future opportunities.

Breaking-down tasks

"Success is the sum of small efforts,
repeated day in and day out."

— Robert Collier

A common problem of procrastination we all face is quiet often not related to time, it has much more to do with our tasks at hand. Take the instance of cleaning up your wardrobe; one look at your huge stack of all the unused things you have collected over time is enough to make you push the task aside. But what if you do not look at the task as completely cleaning your wardrobe? Instead choose to pick one compartment in it. Decide to spend the next 10 minutes cleaning that compartment alone. Once you are done, go away and set your mind on something else, like water the plants, or cook. Come back later and spend another 10 minutes on another compartment. Follow the routine until you have completed all the compartments in your wardrobe.

By breaking down that daunting activity into smaller manageable tasks you make it simpler to digest and act on. Activities that seem difficult and complicated should be divided into smaller doable tasks, this way you avoid feeling stressed about the activity as a whole and can achieve more by focussing on little parts each step of the way. Sooner than you know it you would have completed the task within time and without procrastination.

Small Task
\+ Small Task
\+ Small Task
= Milestone

Milestone
\+ Milestone
\+ Milestone
= Goal Achieved

The essential to succeed in life is in clearly understanding what you can do, how you can do it and do it well. Focus helps you achieve greater heights, but it doesn't come easy. It takes time and effective time management.

"Time management is about life management."

— Idowu Koyenikan

❑

4.
Setting Life Right

"Who you are tomorrow begins with
what you do today."

— Tim Fargo

What do you want to achieve?

Up until now, we have covered the need for the right attitude, the necessary habits to succeed, and the power of the mind and will. So far you are on the right path but only if you know what is it you want to achieve?

What is your END GOAL in mind?

Clarity of an end goal will ensure you map your life in the right direction. No race can ever be carried out if the athletes are unaware of where the finish line is. To gain clarity in life you have to know what are the things you want to achieve that compliment your skills and satisfy your desire for a fulfilled life. Don't be afraid to think beyond your current capacity, nothing is out of reach.

The body is capable of achieving great heights; it is the mind that most often limits it.

What is that ideal aspiration you dream of for yourself?

Too Big

Most dreams remain unachieved because we underestimate the power within us. We undermine our capabilities and abandon our goals. Our search for approval from the world is a constant struggle that makes us conform to its standards, ideals, and construct. Following the herd is another fact that keeps us stuck in our comfort zone and gives us little space to explore or experiment.

Don't look for approval from the world; you can be the next Sachin of cricket or the Prime Minister of our country or even the first human to build a home on Mars; you get the gist. It is your life ultimately; no one knows what you are capable of, but you!

Try try try!

"Every accomplishment starts with the decision to try."

— John F. Kennedy

Your dreams and aspirations can be achieved only when you take the first step towards it. If you want financial freedom in the future you have to start financial planning today. The further you postpone it the slimmer the chances of you achieving it. Yes! Sometimes our goals do seem unattainable, but that should not stop you from taking the first step towards trying to achieve it.

Fear

Then comes fear; the fear of failure makes us lose our nerve and give up on our dreams. One should know how to turn this crippling fear into motivation. Fear is nothing but another emotion, just like happiness or love. We empower fear and give it control of our lives, which is when it interferes with our achievements. The fear of failure blocks our progress towards achieving what we endeavour.

Turn fear into motivation by not letting it 'stop' you, but encourage you instead. Let the fear of failing your exam make you study even harder. Let the fear of a dying business make you work longer to find ways to revive it. Treat fear like an alert sign that is showing you where your mind thinks you lack and may need assistance, approval, or reaffirmation.

Don't let fear cripple you, let it propel you.

— Rajesh Yadav

So you have determined what you want and have overcome fear that prevented you from leaping towards your goals. Then comes the vital question…

How do you plan to achieve it?

A goal without a plan can only be a dream that seizes to turn into reality. Planning is as essential as having goals in life. It gives life direction and meaning.

How can one plan to succeed?

Focus

Starve your distractions, feed your focus.

— Daniel Goleman

Our desire for a different life, for a different self and for better circumstances can come true only if our desires are followed by actions. Our commitment to acting on our dreams and goals is called 'focus'. Through focus we block out all the noise that distracts us from achieving what we want.

You want to own a Mercedes, but are short of a few zeros in your account? Continue to focus on your dream to own the Mercedes, avoid the distraction to spend your hard-earned cash on frivolous inessentials. If you are focussed enough to achieve your goal, your mind will be fixated on it and will be too occupied to give way to hurdles, possible failures or the world telling you otherwise. Write it down, paste a picture on your board, dream of already owning it, and enjoying it.

Don't let your mind drift. When you set a goal with a target in mind, stick to it, be devoted to it and work towards it. Don't let your goals get side-lined because you did not pay heed to it.

Make a plan of how you are going to get what you want. The more detailed a plan, the more likely you are to follow it and see it through. Chalk out every minute step you can possibly think of that could help you on the way to achieving a goal. Focus along with constant reminders and positive affirmations will ensure you achieve what you have set out to do.

Your focus will determine your success.

When do you plan to achieve it?

Ever heard the idiom God is in the details? Well it honestly involves the devil but we like to focus on the good. This idiom speaks of opportunities that evolve from being precise, planned, and prepared. It opens up inroads to creativity and allows you to discover new avenues you may have unheard of.

People do not stumble upon success, they make it happen. One may spend months or years in honing skills, refining attitudes and mastering moves to reach a goal. Sachin Tendulkar, Viswanathan Anand, P.V Sindhu and many more have toiled hard to make their mark in their respective sport. Their success would not have been possible if they did not follow daily schedules to practice till perfect. Unless you chalk out a plan to succeed you will be shooting in the dark and most likely at a moving target.

Make a plan. It does not have to be written in stone. It can change, evolve, and adapt. A plan will give direction and discipline to your dedication, and that is the route you need to take to succeed.

Habits for success

People who enjoy success in their lives can be easily distinguished in a crowd. They are the ones with attitudes that are tuned to attract success. How do they develop such strong attitudes?

Attitudes are nothing but our routine habits formed by the reoccurring thoughts and obsessions. Reoccurring processes become habits and practiced habits turn into an attitude. Your choice of habits will speak volumes about your possibilities to succeed in life. Choose your habits wisely.

"If your habits don't line up with your dream, then you need to either change your habits or change your dream."

— John C. Maxwell

Stress

Be aware of dangerous situations that can affect your health and state of mind. One such situation is living in the past. What has been done in the past cannot be undone. Holding on to mistakes, anger or missed opportunities will only stress you out further. There is nothing good that can come out of living in the past besides knowledge and awareness. Let the past be a learning curve for the future.

Let go of animosity for actions of the past and look towards progress in future. Avoid things, topics, or people that instigate you, or rub you up the wrong way. Not everything is in our control, accept that, and move away while you weed out the negative vibes and make room for positive growth.

Learn from past actions, habits, or interactions that may have pulled you back or pushed you down. Find triggers that initiate these behaviours and avoid their reoccurrence. You have the power to make a change in the things you can control. Change your mindset, your apprehensions, your actions, and reflexes. These tiny tweaks can bring a colossal turn in the way you behave, act, and react.

Stress can be good; it is like fuel to your actions. Some people perform better under stress, especially those who tend to procrastinate often. Understand how your mind and body react when utterly stressed; learn to sight those triggers that alert you of upcoming panic. Knowledge and control over your own emotions and reactions can help you get a handle on stressful situations and easily overcome it.

"If the problem can be solved why worry?
If the problem cannot be solved worrying
will do you no good."

— Shantideva

The learning curve

To succeed, nothing can be more essential than to prepare oneself for success. A great source of learning is feeding yourself with knowledge through constant learning. Experience is a great teacher but wisdom makes your experience worthwhile.

The learning curve should never end, take time out periodically to teach yourself something new. Constant learning lets you keep an open mind to life and its opportunities.

Identify your strength and weaknesses, make notes of your qualities and resources. Understand yourself inside out before you take the leap to make a change for success.

Be open; open to feedback and constructive criticism. Accept what you cannot control and tweak a change to what you can. Graciously accept help when offered and needed, even if you think it could make you look weak.

Take on new challenges and focus on results, not failures. Even failures can bring about positive results that can teach you volumes.

Manage the routine in your life before your routine life begins to manage you.

"Intellectual growth should commence at birth and cease only at death."

— Albert Einstein

❑

Thought-Provoking Questions To Ponder On

- Who you are?
- What would you want to become?
- How much you want to earn?
- What do you want to own?
- Where do you want to live?
- Do you sleep like a baby every night?
- Do you value your time?
- What is your END GOAL in mind?
- What is that ideal aspiration you dream of for yourself?
- How can you plan to succeed?

PART 3: KEYS TO BETTER COLLABORATION

1.
The Secrets of Communication

"Communication – the human connection – is the key to personal and career success."

— Paul J. Meyer.

We humans communicate to share our knowledge, ideas and information. Be it verbal or otherwise, the success of communication depends on the receiver's clarity in understanding the communicated message. The ability to clearly communicate your ideas and thoughts is an essential that can help you succeed in life. Successful people are usually excellent communicators and have the ability to drive and steer conversations that are insightful and stimulating.

"Communication works for those who work at it."

— John Powell

All things being equal, an individual's communication skills and leadership capabilities will distinguish him or her from a crowd onto a path to success.

Your clarity in communication does play a vital role in defining the level of your success. Here are a few do's and don'ts to guide on how to best start conversations.

First impressions matter

People take less than 7 seconds to evaluate a person when they first meet. Within seconds a first impression is formed. So, before you have even said Hello! a person has already decided if you are trustworthy, attractive and worthy of their time. Within split seconds you need to make a powerful impact how will you do that?

Body language: The way you approach a person speaks volumes of the direction of the conversation will take. A person with close folded hands or with hands in their pockets are portraying the message that they are either shy, uncomfortable or not interested in meeting the other. Crouched or turtled shoulders reveals the person is anxious or unconfident. The best way to approach someone is with open body language, hands in the open and shoulders upright and at ease. The right way to begin a conversation with a stranger is to break the ice by beginning with a smile and a chirpy Hello!

Handshakes: A weak handshake is often linked to a person who is shy, uninterested or even incompetent. On the other hand a long handshake can lead to an awkward start to a conversation. A firm handshake, that is not too tight and lasts for no more than 2 seconds works perfectly as a strong introduction.

Eye contact: The key to being an exceptional communicator involves having conversations that lasts. The only way to have meaningful conversations is by getting involved, interacting and reciprocating. You simply cannot have a conversation with an individual and not look at them. Avoiding eye contact can make you come across as inattentive, insincere and sometimes even unattractive. People who maintain eye contact during a conversation are usually perceived as confident, trustworthy and intelligent. But this does not mean you begin a staring competition right away. Ensure you maintain eye contact from time to time to let the person know you are listening and are interested.

Personal space: One of the barriers to communication is the lack of understanding of personal space. There are etiquettes to be followed and maintained when meeting people both formally and informally. Invading personal space is one of the top most criteria that should be followed. Maintaining a 4 feet distance with new acquaintances in a formal setting with a smile and a firm yet short handshake is appropriate. For an informal gathering the rules vary depending on the situation, occasion and personal comfort zones.

Distractions: Research proves that on average a person checks his phone 90 to 100 times a day. In our virtual worlds we are so use to notifications, messages and calls that a ping of the phone automatically catches our attention, sometimes more like a subconscious reflex. During a conversation it is rude to keep checking your phone or sending texts. Such distractions send the message that you have better things to do rather than be a part of the conversation. Pay attention and be present and wholeheartedly when you are having a conversation.

"Communication works for those who work at it."

— John Powell

The ability to speak a language fluently does not make you a good communicator. You may be fluent in English or any other language, but that does not mean you are able to convey your thoughts and ideas with such clarity that people can understand. English here is merely a language while communication is a skill. Until this skill set has been mastered you cannot be an effective communicator.

"Communication is your ticket to success, if you pay attention and learn to do it effectively."

— Theo Gold

Let us focus on some important aspects of communication that we need to inculcate to better the way we present ourselves.

Influence

The ability to convince people goes beyond the use of language or speech. Our methodology to convey our thoughts and ideas is made up of 7% of verbal communication, the rest of the speaking is done from a visual point of view of body posture, style of speaking, accent, facial expressions, physical movements and so on. It is like a package deal, the deal will not be accepted if some parts of the package or offer is missing. Your language skills may be great but your voice modulation may obstruct your message from reaching the audience. You may want to speak about something very important but your body language says you are casual and not serious about the conversation, diluting the seriousness of the message you want to pass on. Your capabilities to integrate a combination of language and behavioural skills to be able to express your ideas effectively, that's what will make you an influencer.

It is more important to influence people than to impress them.

— Adrian Rogers

Anxiety

The art of building conversations is not everybody's cup of tea. Sometimes people get anxious when confronted with the opportunity to speak to someone new or to even say a few words in public. This anxiety culminates from apprehensions and fears that we have within us. Fortunately, most of these apprehensions develop from fears that are preconceived and baseless. With a little persistence and action we can overcome these fears.

Take for instance the fear of speaking in public, to overcome this fear the right action would be to take up an opportunity that encourages you to go out and give a speech to 30 people. Yes, there will be anxiety and a high probability of you messing up as well. But, once the task is complete, you will realize that speaking in public is not as difficult as you imagined it to be.

"Without fear there cannot be courage."

— Christopher Paolini

Set an intention

A conversation that is driven by intent will deliver more value. Before you step into a meeting, an event or a social gathering take a few moments to set an intent which defines what it is you want to derive from this interaction. Do you want to increase your network of business connections, pitch a product or simply mingle with like-minded people to have a good time. Whatever the intention behind the interaction, ensure you are aware of what you want to get out of it, even if it implies just having a good time. This method of intentional conversations will keep you in control guiding every conversation and ensuring meaningful interactions without awkward pauses or absurd small talk.

"All great acts are ruled by intention.
What you mean is what you get."

— Brenna Yovanoff

Be open

Every interaction you have be it a formal business deals with partners or an informal discussions with friends, each needs to be given equal importance. Your openness to let others convey their thoughts and ideas and be heard brings a sense of approachability and receptiveness to the conversation. Being accessible and approachable gives birth to new dialogue that could generate new ideas and open up a whole new world of possibilities.

Take for instance your reluctance to switch jobs. You have been working for an organization for a decade and have received meagre raise in income and see no growth. But the fear of moving from you comfort zone and switching jobs keeps you from going for interviews. Consider a recruiter approaches you of an opportunity that pays better and helps you grow up the corporate ladder, will you be open to hear about the offer? Or will your fear of change stop you from even considering it for even a moment?

"Those who cannot change their minds cannot change anything."

— George Bernard Shaw

Listen actively

People hate the feeling of being ignored in a conversation. If the person you are speaking too is constantly checking his watch or phone or is distracted with things happening in his surroundings then the conversation is definitely going to get one-sided and eventually come to an abrupt halt. Here you are non-verbally signalling that you are uninterested in this dialogue even if you are consciously interested. Active listening is one vital part of having meaningful conversations. One-way communication where you speak about what is important to you and the other speaks about what matters to him, both being on a different tangent the conversation will naturally lead to no proper conclusion.

To actively listen one must ensure he or she is totally invested in the moment with zero distractions. Eye contact and positive body language will aid the conversation taking it to newer heights. From complicated sales pitches to simple dinner at home with the family, every conversation must have your complete focus and dwell on the idea of knowing or learning more.

"Most of the successful people I've known are the ones who do more listening than talking."

— Bernard Baruch

We have covered the do's and don'ts and the important aspects of clear communication. All of these were more from listening and reciprocation point of view. Let us delve a little deeper to actionable insights that if inculcated can make you a better collaborator.

Know yourself. What are you good at? How do other people perceive you? Are you friendly, accessible and open or are you closed, choosy and reserved? Understanding the core of who you are and the perception others have of you will give you a better understanding of how you should approach people.

For example, if you colleagues find you reserved, take up the opportunity to walk up and start a conversation with a fellow worker, even if it is just small talk. Smile and greet others on your way in or out. Take one step at a time, with a few tiny tweaks to change your image in the minds of others. Slowly but surely you will see they begin to become more receptive and open to your ideas, thoughts and conversations. This key step is the first step to building bridges of collaboration.

Being open is one part of the solution; the other is going out of your way to meet them halfway. Remember conversations are a two way street. This includes being open to understanding their side of the conversation, suggestions and point of view. Your openness to accepting your shortcomings and respecting their opinions to make a change, will only make you stronger and wiser. Attention and respect are two value propositions that anybody is willing to receive with open arms especially when joining forces for a common cause. If you are setting up a business or merely gathering for a social cause, in both scenarios if you are open and willing to respect and inculcate the opinions of others in key decision making processes you will have them deeply invested in the cause that you both are working towards.

The effectiveness of communication can be measured on the basis of the output. Collaborations that emerge from conversations require a lot of skill, practice and learning. Closing huge business deals or convincing your kid to buy a health snack instead of a chocolate, each requires a skill set of understanding your audience, driving your intention and clearly communicating your thoughts in ways that are effective and impactful.

"Communication – the human connection – is the key to personal and career success."

— Paul J. Meyer

❑

2.
The Relationship Formula

We humans live in groups; our entire lives revolve around our families, work and social gatherings. In our interconnected life we need to maintain good relationships with others to be able to stay happy, peaceful and live fulfilled lives. Relationships here play a major role in maintaining this peace and fulfilment.

"Relationships are built on the bedrock of trust and acceptance."

— Rajesh Yadav

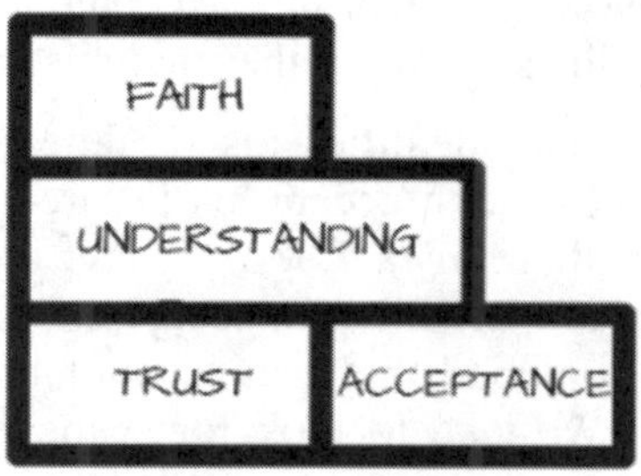

Me and myself

But before we deep dive into our relationship with others we need to first comprehend our relationship with ourselves. This refers to our acceptance of who we are and our capabilities.

Who am I?
What are my values?
What are my strengths and weaknesses?
What are my goals and dreams?

Understanding yourself and accepting who you are is the basis of building strong relationships. It is only when you know yourself will you be open to understanding others and connecting with them.

Take for instance, Kumar is an excellent salesman. He hits all his targets at work and never fails to achieve the goals set for him, no matter how tough. He has a way with words and building strong relationships that has got him so far. Unfortunately, one of Kumar's weaknesses is that he cannot grasp technology. At work, he has to work with and depend on systems and software to ensure his work is fed into the system and up-to-date. His inability to keep up with the technical aspects of his work is soon becoming an issue. His boss has tried to bring up the topic of his technical inabilities and find ways to assist him work around it, but Kumar seems to get defensive and annoyed whenever the topic is brought up. Why? Plainly because, Kumar does know his failure to comprehend technology; he hasn't accepted his weakness and thus keep blaming the software rather than his incompetence.

Only when Kumar identifies his weakness and realizes his mistakes, will he be able to accept his failure and work towards making it his strength. Many a times, we have disagreements with people because we are unwilling to accept our shortcomings. The rage we feel when somebody holds us accountable for our mistakes usually blinds us. We tend to look for scapegoats to throw the blame on, just like Kumar who blames glitches in technology for his incompetence.

"The worst loneliness is to not be comfortable with yourself."

— Mark Twain

Our relationship with ourselves, our own mind and bodies needs to be strong. This means knowing your strengths and accepting your weaknesses.

Strengths

Take a moment to sit down and think about things that you are good at. You may be street-smart, you could be great at DIY's and fixing things, you could be artistic and have an exceptional voice.

What are those things that make you, you?

I am good at ....
I am better at ....
I am great at ....

Once you have listed your strengths you will have a clearer outlook towards life. You will have a better ideas of which path to choose as a career based on your abilities. You will realize what kind of people you need to surround yourself with. If you are a bubbly person, you need to surround yourself with equally energetic and happy people who match your vibe. If you are a thinker and prefer soul-talk, you will want to stick with intellectuals rather than over-energetic youth. An awareness of your abilities and strengths will help you choose the right career path, friends and partners.

Weaknesses

Intermingled with strengths are your weaknesses. We all have our unique weaknesses and have to deal with it in our own ways. What is important is to identify your weaknesses and accept them. More often than never weaknesses are linked to failure, due to which people fear accepting it.

Anu was a smart woman and had already reached the peak of her career by the time she was 28. She was earning a 6 digit monthly income and was incharge of a lot of responsibilities at work, which she seamlessly seemed to handle. Anu's strengths definitely were far beyond her weaknesses, but she had one part of her life in which she failed miserably. She failed to handle her finances well. She was spending more than she earned on things she didn't need but nevertheless wanted. By the end of each month Anu was left with little or nothing in her bank account.

For a young person, earning a handsome salary and with no dependents this was unacceptable. Her parents tried to discuss this with her on many occasions, but Anu had never failed in any part of her life before and refused to accept that she was failing in correcting her financial choices. As time passed by, a personal medical reason made Anu quit her job and she was left nearly penniless after paying her medical and healthcare bills. It was at that low point in her life when Anu realised her failure and began working towards prudence in financial matters. What are your weaknesses?

I cannot ...
I am not good at ...
I am terrible at ...

Once you have acknowledged your weakness it is time you accept it even when people point it out to you. Don't take things personally rather use those opportunities to further investigate; find ways to turn your weaknesses into strengths.

To fall in love with yourself is the first secret to happiness.

— Robert Morley

Me and others

Establishing a strong understanding of your own capabilities and weaknesses gives you a strong foundation to build lasting relationships with other. Once you are comfortable in your own skin you begin to realise that things that other people say and do which use to bug you earlier now don't. Your acceptance of your shortcomings allows you to sincerely acknowledge it even when others point it out to you, therefore it does not become a point of argument, but rather a point of discussion that could help you better understand ways to overcome your weakness.

Being open is one way of building strong relationships with people. People like to engage with others who they can easily know and trust. Openness in relationships and communications helps build trust and inculcates a sense of commitment from the other to reciprocate with an equivalent amount of openness.

Here are a few traits that you should inculcate to enable you build stronger relationships.

Stay Grounded

Everybody has that one friend on their list who loves to brag about himself/herself. Usually, that person will be found at the bottom of everyone's friends list. Relationships are a series of give and take, no matter what the setup is; from official connections to social groups there always needs to be an equal level of giving and receiving. Self-centred people who always speak about themselves, their ideas, their experiences, without giving others a listening ear will soon have no one to speak with. Pride can be one reason for such behaviour. To build a strong relationship one must keep pride aside.

This reminds me of an anecdote, the flowing river was filled with pride for she carried the sweetest water and travelled from far off mountains across states and to the mighty sea. In all her pride she noticed a well and began to brag, "Hey well, look where I come, high mountains and dangerous valleys and flow to the strong sea and look at you, stuck in one place with nowhere to go." The calm well chirpily retorted, "Oh yes! Dear river, you are immensely beautiful and strong, but look what has become of you. You travel so far and wide that your waters have become filthy and finally you flow into the sea where you water turns salty and of no use to humanity. While I, although stagnant am filled with sweet water that is immensely purposeful to those who depend on my water and find it difficult to survive without me."

Pride has no place in a relationship unless used to stand up suppressed. Stay grounded and treat people the way you want them to treat you.

Be like a tree. Stay grounded, keep growing,
and know when to let go.

— Unknown

Build Trust

People that are not trustworthy fail to build relationships that last. Trust is one of the pillars for long-lasting relationships. Consider marriage, two partners stick together for life, sharing their deepest desires and open up their vulnerabilities because they trust that no matter what happens their partner will always have their back. A salesman in a large organization is able to pitch and sell a product worth 10 crores without any apprehension, even though his own net worth is barely 10% of that amount, because he trusts his organization and management has the capacity to deliver on their promise. If you are not trustworthy or distrust the person you are trying to build a relationship with, then expect it to be a brief episodic association.

This reminds me of a passed on anecdote. On a flight that was airborne and had hit a patch of rough skies, the flight attendant was struggling to keep the passengers calm. The turbulence was outrageous and every passenger was scared praying for their safety. Through all of this chaos a little boy who seemed to be travelling by himself, sat near the window looking out without a sense of fear or panic. The gentleman next to him was astonished at his behaviour. Soon the turbulence was over, the weather calmed down and the flight returned to clear skies. The inquisitive gentlemen asked the boy how he remained so calm in spite of the situation around him. He simply replied that the pilot who was flying the plane was his father and he had faith in his father that he would not let anything happen to him.

Relationships are built on foundations of faith and trust. The stronger the faith the longer lasting will be the relationship. Trust and honesty in personal and work relationships builds powerful bonds.

Avoid Assumptions

As humans we have an imaginative mind and tend to build up stories in our minds. These stories revolve around ourselves and the people we interact with. It is okay to have a creative mind, but it gets dangerous when start to misjudge these concocted mind fiction as facts. These fictional stories are usually doles out as judgements and assumptions.

'I think this may have happened hence he or she did this.' How many times you have built up scenarios like this in your mind and judge a person's behaviour? Assumptions like these tend to bring doubt, cynicism and mistrust in a relationship. Nobody likes to be judged. So avoid assumptions.

As we discussed in the earlier chapter, communication is a two-way street. Be open and straightforward; seek clarification to understand the situation and the reason behind the action. Let your relationship be void of any unnecessary misconceptions. The more you communicate with your partner or co-worker the better the stronger the relationship will grow. And above all under all circumstances, avoid judgement from baseless assumptions.

If in doubt, ask.

Be mindful

Being aware of your surroundings and the people who are a part of it is necessary. Be wary of the conversations you have and more importantly how you communicate the messages you want to convey. This piece of information comes in handy when you are stuck in conversations that are difficult, like when you have to break bad news, or tell someone something that could possibly hurt their feelings. The best way around it is to be mindful towards their feelings. This need not mean you should sugar-coat your conversation, but rather find ways and means to put across your message in a more tactful way that is easily digestible by the receiver.

Take the example of an employee at work who has terrible body odour and you have received a lot of complaints from colleagues who sit around that employee. You have to act on the situation even though it is tough and can possibly be taken in a harsh way. The better way to approach this situation is to understand a little about the person, does he have a medical condition or is he travelling under a difficult condition which makes him sweat and thus the odour? Clarity of the situation will give you a better perspective and offer advice in terms of an actionable proposition rather than an acquisition.

Say it is a medical condition that the employee is suffering from here you could empathise with the persona and offer to suggest a good doctor that could assist him overcome his medical problem. Empathy goes a long way and so does a little bit of mindfulness, it shows you care about the person and the relationship.

Nobody likes to be lonely. Our lack of care and disconnection from relationships is the reason for loneliness. Self-centered people are often the ones who find themselves alone. Relationships that evolve from mere acquaintances to a one of closeness filled with compassion, care and empathy are the ones that are strongest and everlasting.

❑

3.
Be SMART

"Either you run the day or the day runs you."
— Jim Rohn

In our previous chapter we discussed the importance of goal setting and how commitment, accountability, self-actualization and milestones help you to set the right goals for your life. In this chapter we go one step ahead to understand the difference between setting goals and setting SMART goals. To find success in everything we do we need to put in a 100% effort.

There are two ways to doing any activity, the hard way and the smart way. Take for example you decide to go river rafting in a flowing stream. Which way do you believe a trained specialist will take you through? Will he take you upstream where you will have to struggle to paddle fighting against the current and constantly struggling to find the right direction? Or will he take you downstream where the flow of the water will let your raft float almost effortlessly, allowing you to merely guide the direction of the raft?

Obviously the smarter route would be going downstream, in the direction of the water allowing you to additionally focus on the thrill and beauty of the journey while you are on that raft journeying towards your destination.

Our efforts determine the possibility of us achieving our goals.

— Rajesh Yadav

Setting goals is the first step towards success, achieving our goals is the final destination. Between goal setting and achieving it there is a ton of effort that needs to be put in, which is hard work. Nothing can be achieved without the right combination of hard and smart work. But before we decide the course of our effort we need to understand what success means to each of us individually.

Achieving financial freedom?
Being Happy?
Success in relationships?
Being in the pink of health?

Take a couple of moments to define your ideas of success. Identify those goals whose achievements would give you true happiness and fulfilment in life? These goals will be your legitimate life goals. Start with broader visions of values like happiness, satisfaction, financial freedom, etc. Then try refining it down to what are the things you want to do that will help you achieve true happiness. If financial freedom is your goal then, what do you need to do to secure you future financially. Write down your thoughts and goals, visualise them.

Working towards a goal can be like the idea of rafting. When you have a goal that excites you and encourages you towards achieving it that's when you put your utmost effort into working in the right direction. Signs of your complete involvement in the process are, you may lose complete track of time and rarely get distracted. You may find even the toughest tasks simple. This proves that you are working in the right direction, which is the flow of the tide, downstream. Remember smart people work downstream.

On the other hand sometimes your goals seem unattainable and the process to achieving it seems tough and dreadful; you probably are working in the wrong direction.

"The most successful men work smart, not hard"
— Bangambiki Habyarimana,

Take for example one of your goals included owning a home in one the posh societies in your city. This home may cost you a bomb, way beyond your budget. You may have to work some extra hours each month for a year to make up the lump-sum for the down payment itself. You begin to work hard month after month and start accumulating the money you need. You reach half way through and now start feeling strained and not as interested. Suddenly you lose the drive to put in those extra hours any longer. You inspect your work and realise you enjoy your job, it is what it has been all this while, but somehow you have lost the excitement you felt earlier. May be here you need to take another look at your set goal, is your goal of owning that posh home still relevant or have you changed your mind? Do you think that maybe that home is not worth the effort you put in?

Life is like a rolling ball, never constant. So are our goals, values and wants, ever changing. If ever you feel like you are working upstream to achieve something, it is time to take a break and re-evaluate your goals and values. In all probability your goals, wants and values are not aligned and hence make you feel stressed out. A course correction can ensure you remain motivated and authentic to your goals and values.

Working smart requires determination along with discernment.

— Rajesh Yadav

Now that you have your goals in place it is time to work on achieving them. Here are some methods you could implement to ensure you achieve your goals in the smartest ways possible.

Creating specific action plans

Prioritising your activities is one of the top most necessities to achieving your gaols. The lack of a plan and prioritising your activities will lead you down a path of uncertainty which defeats the purpose of setting goals. It is like driving towards a destination, you know where you want to go and by when you want to reach there but you do not have the map that shows you how to get to your destination, in time.

A clear and specific plan will define what your goal is and the roadmap to get there. Your will set a timeline to your achievement. You will set milestones along the way and while you achieve each milestone it guarantees you to stay on the right path to success. A specific plan will give you a deadline that works as a constant reminder to work towards what you have set out to do. Be clear with your thought and plans and define the tiniest details and the necessary steps to get there. The more detailed your plan the easier it is to achieve your goal.

Give me six hours to chop down a tree and
I will spend the first four sharpening the axe.

— Abraham Lincoln

Managing time and schedules

Every smart worker knows that time is vital, especially when you are creating something of value. Scheduling your commitments based on priorities is the basis of time management. Each of us has been given an equal number of hours each day, how we use it speaks volumes of what we will achieve. Make it a habit to schedule your plan for the next day in advance. This lets you get a drift of what are your priority assignments and to-do's that need to be accomplished. Preparing a task list the previous day gives you time to subconsciously prepare yourself for the tasks ahead, ensuring that you are completely immersed in the activity giving it your 100%.

Pre-planning also gives you clarity of what you have in-store and avoid cramming things in your to-do list that are of least priority. For example, you have a project that you are working on and is going to take you all day to complete it. Your boss walks in and hands you over a task that needs to be completed before end of day.

Since you had planned in advance you know that you have your hands full with the project which is priority. Avoid multitasking if you are not good at it. Multitasking requires high efficiency and attention. It is okay to say 'No' to ensure you do not over burden yourself. Over scheduling tasks and over burdening yourself will only lead to burn-out, leaving you feeling incompetent and stressed.

"If you want to make good use of your time,
you've got to know what's most important
and then give it all you've got."

— Lee Iacocca

Accept help

Be open to assistance whenever needed. Asking your team members for help does not mean that you are incapable or unworthy; it just means that the work is not top on your priority list of other things to-do.

Success is not always a single person's effort, it usually requires a team. The more open you are with your teammates, the better the chances of you'll working in tandem with each other. Teamwork can be difficult, it is like a dance, in the beginning each of you are learning your steps at your own pace and beat. But, once each of you has mastered the steps and the beats then you are tuned into the rhythm and a beautiful dance unfolds.

"You can do two things at once, but you can't focus effectively on two things at once."

— Gary Keller

Take a break to re-energize

Just like a used battery, nothing fruitful can be expected of someone who is physically and emotionally drained. To work smart you need to be at your best at all times. Burning the night oil before an crucial exam or presentation will only make you feel drained and exhausted during the actual exam or presentation. To ensure you are on top of your game take breaks and regain your energy. These could be short breaks during the day, quick weekend trips in a month or month off during a year. How much ever time it may take you to relax and re-energize, ensure you take these breaks to cool off.

Just as distance makes the heart grow fonder, similarly time-off from the mundane will give you that satisfaction of being distanced from the activity yet keep you attuned to return to it with a fresh outlook, be it work or otherwise.

"Taking a break can lead to breakthroughs."
— Russell Eric Dobda

Look for shortcuts

Working smart does not always mean finding the shorter route to success, but sometimes it does mean find a workaround to speed up the process. En route to achieving your goals you will have to work long and hard to get there, but sometimes a detour could help you speed up the activity and to get you to your destination.

For instance, two employees have been given a task to create a presentation for the boss within the next 3 hours. They need to curate the data, do a little bit of research and make a presentation that looks professional enough to present to the board of directors. The first employee spends the first hour finding the right colour scheme, look and feel and then moves on to mining data and doing some research. The second employee picks up a readymade template from a professional presentation template site within the first 10 minutes and begins to spend the rest of the time on research and curating data. Then both of them submitted their presentation on time, but which of them worked smartly? The second off-course because he prioritised his work allotting little time to mundane and more to quality work like data and research. All things being equal the quality of his presentation has to be far more superior.

"The early bird gets the first worm, but the wisest bird gets the fastest one."
— Matshona Dhliwayo

Do no procrastinate

Every human has this innate tendency to procrastinate. Procrastination refers to our activity of putting off a task at hand

and delaying its completion. Sometime we procrastinate due to pure laziness and the other times due to fear of the task at hand. Smart workers understand the hindrance that procrastination can be and learn to keep a check on their tendency to procrastinate.

The simplest way to avoid procrastination would be to find out what are its key drivers, in other words the distractions. Find out what are the things that you tend to do when you procrastinate. Do you end up spending time on social media, keep clicking the snooze button to avoid waking up or take up some other activities instead.

Whatever your distraction, track it and try to weed it out from you surrounding when you sit to get that task done. If you intend to wake up at 6 am each morning to go for a jog and have been hitting that snooze button every time the alarm went off you will never be able to get out of bed and jog. Realising that the snooze button is the hindrance is the first step. Eliminate the hindrance by keeping your alarm clock further away from you. This way you will be forced out of bed to switch or snooze the clock which is sure to wake you up and get you up and about. Now that you are up and awake how about a jog!

"Work hard,
and you will earn good rewards.
Work smart,
and you will earn great rewards.
Work hard and work smart, and you will earn
extraordinary rewards."

— Matshona Dhliwayo

❑

4.
Reset your Life

"When the going gets tough, the tough get going."
— Jim Rohn

Tough times come and go like the weather, it never lasts. But tough people do.

Have you done enough during your time here on earth to strengthen yourself to face life's challenges? The key lies in not spending time, but how you spend investing it.

In the past chapters, we have discussed the power of the mind and will, our attitude and need for confidence. We also discussed the essential habits needed to succeed in life and the key factors that can be implemented to make a change. But, unless you unleash your willingness to spur a change, all of these acts will remain a mere one-time activity without any influence or impact on your life.

You have heard the quote, 'Time is money'. Here 'Money' is never the goal; it is a mere bi-product of time well spent. Each of us is gifted with the same 24 hours each day, an equal amount to everyone alive. Yet, some of us seem to fritter time away, linger or spend it in procrastination while the rest seem to find that the time at hand is just not enough for the things they have intentionally set out to do. Why so? It is about our perspective on life.

What are you spending most of your time on?

Does your day of leisure involve your couch, a lot of junk food and hours of binge-watching your favourite series?

Remember, ultimately we are the sum of what we spend most of our time on. Successful people are busybodies. They seem to have no time for frivolous activities. Every minute of their day is pre-scheduled and every activity has a purpose. Be it a jog in the park for exercise or a networking lunch with a potential client, there is intent in every activity they participate in. Activities with intent require your complete attention and warrant your full-potential.

Successful people form the habit of doing thing that failure don't like to do.

"Progress is impossible without change,
and those who cannot change their minds
cannot change anything."

— George Bernard Shaw

So, the obvious question arises: Are you willing to change? If your answer is yes, then its time you exposed your true potential to maximize every moment you live. Why then do we fail to apply our full potential in everything we do? The most probable reason could be because you are not inspired enough. So then,

What inspires you?

Find the things that you are most likely to do without the need for a push, a reminder or procrastination. Jot them done. These are the activities that you are likely to do with your complete potential. Do more of it.

Be aware of your activities during the day, pre-plan your day and try to ensure each activity has an intention affixed to it. If you have scheduled a leisure time to read during the day, try to either spend it by switching off your phone and access to social media. Spend that time completely absorbed in reading and nothing else. Be committed to what you do.

Focus on what you want

We spend most of our time running away from things we want to avoid. Our negativity gets the better of us and pulls us away from what we should be doing. Rerun the conversations you had during the day, does it have more negative connotations to it?

I don't want to be poor. I hate my job.
I don't want this person in my life.

We need to rid ourselves of this negativity and bring about a positive outlook in everything we do. If you hate your job, then think about what your dream job looks like and what you need to do to be eligible for it. Spend time working towards the things you want, rather than running away from the things you don't want. Our minds are a powerhouse, what we believe is what we get. If we believe we are not good enough, we will receive negative vibes and it holds us back.

Look for inspiration and challenges in daily life, you never know what could spur you to do things you were once uninterested in. Take the example of Sir Edmund Hillary, as a teen on a school trip to Mount Ruapehu where he was exposed to climbing realised he had the endurance and strength far beyond most of the teens of his age. He realised his potential and began to put it to use.

He finished his first successful climb to the peak of Mount Ollivier in 1939. His love for mountaineering knew no bounds and so he chose the profession of a beekeeper which gave him the freedom to travel and climb during the summers. He successfully climbed New Zealand's highest peak Mount Cook, Switzerland's

Alps and has his eyes set on Mount Everest. His first expedition was a failure in 1951. But on his second expedition in May of 1953, Edmund reached the summit of Mount Everest, making him the first person to reach the summit of Mount Everest.

When asked about his failure the first time around, Edmund replied saying he had affixed his sight on that peak. In his belief what he had over the mountain was that the mountain had stopped growing at its peak 29,035 feet, but his will continued to grow stronger to accomplish this feat.

> *"Our greatest glory is not in never falling, but in rising every time we fall."*
>
> ***— Confucius***

Be Confident

Confidence is more of an ability than an attitude. Your ability to carry out a task or an activity seamlessly knowing you will not fail at it is your confidence. While confidence can be called an attitude, the lack of ability can demolish confidence. Your success depends on a combination of your confidence and ability or in other words discipline. If you are confident about your job at hand, you will do it with ease. If you are disciplined about your tasks at work, you will ultimately achieve perfection in what you do. Hence, your confidence mingled with self-discipline is likely to make you successful in whatever you do.

The attitude of persistence is necessary to strengthen your capabilities. Think of it this way, you are overweight and need to lose 30 kgs to gain the right body mass index. You begin a regime of exercising an hour each day and follow a strict diet given to you by your dietician. You work-out and control your diet for 3 weeks and see results. You continue the rigorous workout but start lagging on the diet in the next few weeks. It starts showing your progress, which is getting slower. Sooner or later over some time you will give up both, due to your lack of persistence.

"Patience, persistence, and perspiration make an unbeatable combination for success."

— Napoleon Hill

Desire deeply

Nothing can stop you from achieving what you desire, but yourself. You hold the key to your desires and the ability to fulfill them. If there is something you want then you need to go get it. That luxurious car, that business deal, the posh home, that job or life partner, no matter what your want may be, if you have a deep desire you are bound to work towards fulfilling it.

Successful people have the ability to clearly define their desires. Their clarity of the objectives helps them gain the foresight to decipher what they need to achieve their wants. And they work hard to build their abilities to help them achieve their desires. A true sense of commitment and responsibility can take you a long way. Know the direction you want your life to take, align your actions to work towards that direction. Be continuously persistent and positive.

In order to succeed, your desire for success should be greater than your fear of failure.

— Bill Cosby

Do not fear

One of the biggest reasons for failure is fear.

- Fear of failure — What if I do not succeed?
- Fear of success — If I succeed will I be able to continue?
- Fear of excess — My expectations are too high, I cannot achieve that.

- Fear of change — Will be able to adapt to the newness?
- Fear of the future — I cannot see what I could possibly do next.
- Fear of pressure — What if I fail, what will people think of me?
- Fear of the unknown — I don't think I should go down that path.

Fear in all its forms continues to guide our every move. Our human mind is tuned to prefer safer options. We subconsciously follow the herd and feel safe hiding our mistakes in the crowd. Those that do not succumb to fear are more likely to taste success at some point. Their ability to shun the herd and move in a direction that they desire motivates them further to achieve what they have set out to do. Consider it this way, a human who goes astray from the crowd will have herd pointing at him waiting for him to fail. If he is strong minded and determined these onlookers will further encourage him to prove himself to the ones who tell him otherwise. It is your outlook to life that matters. If you have a strong will and deep desire, your confidence and abilities will automatically lead you to success.

"I make more mistakes than anyone else I know, and sooner or later, I patent most of them."

— Thomas A. Edison

In our previous chapters, we discussed how fear can be overcome with introspection, self-assessment and belief and above all by keeping a check on our emotions. Let not fear cripple your ability to perform. Take tiny steps towards what you want to achieve and face your fears with persistence and practicality.

One step at a time

Too much of anything can be overwhelming and indigestible. Do not look at a goal or success as a whole; you are most likely going to be intimidated by its mere idea. Instead, plan your journey towards your goal into multiple smaller ones.

If Navin wants to be financially secure by the age of 40 and decides to start being prudent with his finances at the age of 30, then achieving financial freedom within the next 10 years may seem like a far-fetched idea. He has calculated his expenses and has arrived at a corpus of ₹ 2 crores which he needs to build over the next decade to be financially stress-free. Navin continues to look at that intimidating figure of ₹ 2 crores which seems an arduous task to achieve. So he decides he needs to focus on smaller amounts that will finally compound into his larger corpus. So for the first year, he decides he has to accumulate 2 lakhs as his first milestone towards the corpus. Now two lakhs doesn't seem as impossible as 2 crores right. Doable!

Every monstrous task that your fear cannot be achieved, can be, if you just take some time out to make a plan to achieve it.

"Great things are not done by impulse, but by a series of small things brought together."

— Vincent Van Gogh

There is no single secret sauce to success. As individuals, each of us are a rare combination of our personalities, traits and unique quirks. It is up to each of us to understand our individual abilities, core strengths and unique values that we imbibe to find ways to put them into practice in our daily lives. Build a career in a field that you enjoy, find a partner that balances and compliments your personality, follow a hobby that inspires you, and enhance the habits that add value to your life. It is in these tiny calculated steps of enriching our life is where we set a strong foundation on which we can build our successful lives.

Envision it. Work it. Get it.

— Rajesh Yadav

❑

Thought-Provoking Questions To Ponder On

- Who am I?
- What are my values?
- What are my strengths and weaknesses?
- What are my goals and dreams?
- What does success means to me?
- Achieving financial freedom?
- Being Happy?
- Success in relationships?
- Being in the pink of health?
- What inspires you?

PART 4: DIRECTING YOUR LIFE'S STORY

1.
Who is In-charge?

"Efforts and courage are not enough without purpose and direction."

—John F. Kennedy

An 18-year-old boy was playing the Ranji Trophy match for Delhi against Karnataka. Being unbeaten as a batsman the previous day, his team depended on his performance the next day. His career depended on his performance the next day. A lot was at stake. The night before this crucial day his 54-year old father suddenly takes ill and passes away. He had two choices, to stay home and grieve until his father's death or to stay strong, walk out that door play for his team and return home for his father's last rites.

Against all odds, he chose the latter. One because it was a crucial match that could make or break his career in cricket and the other, being his father's dream to see him as an established cricketer playing for his country. Needless to say, he played well in spite of his grief. He batted his best, scoring 90 runs that took his team out of the danger zone and back on track. After being struck out he returned to the dressing room, removed his gear, and headed home to perform his father's last rites.

His determination, efforts, and courage have made him a renowned name in Indian cricket today - Virat Kohli. Haven't you heard of him too? This 18-year-olds life changed that day because he made a choice based not only on effort or courage but on purpose and determination. He has learned to channel his skill, aggression, and efforts in the right direction making him a sought after player in the world of cricket.

What are you determined to accomplish in your life?

Steer your life

Having direction and purpose in life is vital. Life is like a large ship sailing across oceans. There has to be a destination that it is bound for. Only right navigation, a well-defined route, and a proper destination will take ensure the ship fulfills the purpose that it has set out for. Start by answering these questions:

What is it you are passionate about?

What is it that you are good at doing?

The intersection

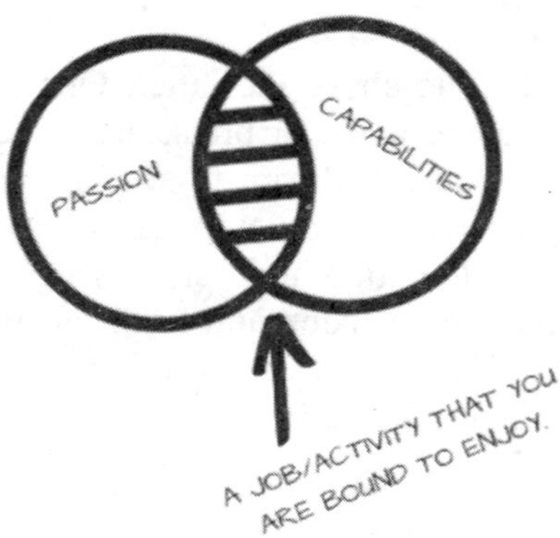

You may have heard many people speak about their work so passionately. The usual words you hear are, 'I don't feel like I have worked a single day in my life.'

How can they say that?

It is their passion for what they are doing that makes them love their job. If you love music and hate physical activities and are asked to spend 2 hours each day on both activities respectively, which 2 hours will feel the longest and which one the shortest? Obviously, exercising will feel like a burden after a couple of minutes, while singing might come more naturally. It is the same in life, the choices we make have to be in tandem with our values, preferences, and capabilities. If either of these is absent then every choice made will feel like swimming against the tide, terribly tedious.

Where does your passion intersect with your capabilities?

Power of the conscious mind

We have discussed the capabilities of our mind in turning our dreams into reality. How the right attitude, strong will power, and a tad bit of confidence can take you places you never imagined yourself to be in.

Your mind is a power house.

Remember the story of the elephant conditioned to believe that a rope could hold him back even when he became way stronger? That's the power of your mind, it can trick you into believing you are incompetent, inefficient, or incapable. But, that same mind if conditioned to believe otherwise can turn around your beliefs and your life. Take the example of Dhirubhai Ambani, a teenager who sold deep-fried snacks for a living, served as a gas station attendant, saved up some money, and slowly built his textile company from scratch. It was his will power to succeed combined with his hard work and a constant eye on his goal that made him reach the exponential level of growth he achieved in his lifetime.

"Pursue your goals even in the face of difficulties and convert adversities into opportunities."

— Dhirubhai Ambani

No matter how unreachable a goal may seem if a person makes up his/her mind to achieve it anything is possible. An actor like Sharukh Khan, an outsider, with no Godfather in the film industry had decided that he was going to rule the city of Mumbai with his work. He had laid down his intention and stuck to his dream. Today, he is one of the most loved Bollywood actors, who is world-famous. He didn't just rule Mumbai but ruled the hearts of multitudes across the globe.

Your desire to succeed cannot be a statement that changes every day as time passes by. It has to be substantial, something that you hold close to your heart.

Statement of intent

Have you got the right intentions?

The majority of human actions are the result of the desire of an individual to take a certain action, and the capacity of an individual to make a conscious decision. In other words:

Productive action is a product of the right intention.

If your mind is tuned to seeing good and being positive, then your busy will follow suit attract good vibes and positivity. Your behaviour and actions are set on the track of your intentions. This is the power of the subconscious mind. The right set of intentions can drive you to success while the wrong ones can drive you to doom.

The choice is yours. Improve your attitude towards life and set intentions, daily. Start your day on a positive note and both mentally and physically. A fresh start to the day gives you a fresh view on your road to success. Exercise both your mind and body. Physical exercise rejuvenates your body and gives it that much-needed adrenaline rush that drives you through the day. A refreshed positive mindsets the right mood to accepts good vibes that keep your mind free from unnecessary stress and overthinking.

Begin your day with positive affirmations. This helps you announce to the universe that you are open to accepting all that is good and fruitful. A short time spent in meditation helps you recalibrate your body and mind, giving you total control over your behaviour and thinking. Meditation creates a sense of mindfulness that can have lasting effects on your belief system.

"The path to success is to take massive, determined action."

— Tony Robbins

Once your thoughts and intentions align, the rest is left to your actions. This part gets tricky because sometimes the mind is willing but the body is not. This is especially true for physical activities. Take for instance you decide you want to start running every morning to stay fit. You need to leave for work by 7.30 am and so you need to wake up by 5 to be able to finish a 30 minute running route and be back in time to get ready for the day ahead.

You have made up your mind, prepared your clothes and shoes, set the alarm clock for 4.45 am. When the alarm rings you wake up remembering you have to go for a jog. But it's a cozy cold morning; it feels like you haven't slept enough to get out of bed just yet. You begin a debate in your mind and by default you hit the snooze button and get snug back under your blanket. You had the right intention but your body was not ready. This habit to 'postpone doing' begins with a small habit like the snooze button on your alarm in the morning and snowballs into your larger activities like updating your CV for an excellent opportunity that awaits your response.

The determination to act immediately needs to be inculcated with a pure understanding of how procrastination can ruin great opportunities.

> *"Feeling sorry for yourself, and your present condition is not only a waste of energy but the worst habit you could possibly have."*
>
> **— *Dale Carnegie***

These tiny changes in your life may not come easy, especially if you have been a pessimist or a procrastinator for a while. Any activity prolonged over a period of time turns into a habit and further down the line becomes a personal trait or attitude. So,

What does it take to make that colossal change to inculcate a winning attitude?

1. Thoughts are just thoughts. Not every thought you have is necessarily the truth in the real world.
2. Concentrate on what you want, not what you don't want.
3. There is a lesson to be learned in every problem you face.
4. Change is the only constant. Do not resist change.
5. Be grateful for all you get and mindful of each human that you know.

6. Give 100% to every conscious act in which you are involved in.
7. We, humans, are imperfect; forgo the illusion that everything has to be perfect.
8. Know yourself. Respect yourself. Know that you are enough.

"The only person who can pull me down is myself, and I'm not going to let myself pull me down anymore."
— C. JoyBell C.

Does it sometimes feel like time is passing by without much change?

Do you feel like you are stuck in a routine where every day passes by without adding any significant value in your life?

You had better be ready to change your mind when needed, or your mind will change you.
—Henry B. Wilsonx

These are signs that you have stopped growing, evolving, and changing. We, humans, have the capability to learn and adapt to the rapid progress that life is making each day. It is our choice to adapt ourselves to this progress or remain in our mundane routines, as life passes us by. Even intelligent people sometimes stop growing, this growth is in terms of adaptability, enthusiasm, receptiveness, and alertness. When we get set in a routine, we get settled in our comfort zone. Our mind and body get accustomed to patterns of activities, work, and family life that make us feel comfortable. Any change in this comfort will shake us up and throw us off track.

It is similar to a person who has been with an organization for over a decade, he has built his comfort zone in the work profile, with his colleagues, in this office environment and everything related to it. When a lucrative job opportunity knocks his door, the thought of breaking the routine and jumping out of the comfort zone scares him, making him skip the opportunity and remain stagnant at where he was. His reluctance to being adaptable or flexible along with his lack of enthusiasm for the new makes him lose out an opportunity that could advance his career and propel his growth.

How many times have you missed opportunities
to upskill yourself?
Have you let go of these opportunities
because you truly lack the time?
Or was it your comfort zone that you were protecting?

Stop resisting

Remember everything in life has a purpose. Some opportunities require you to come out of your comfort zone and stretch your wings, while others may not. That being said one must stop focusing on the 'have not' and rather on the 'have'.

A recently graduated student is in the market frantically looking for a job to start his career. The market scenario is bad, economies have tumbled and hiring is at an all-time low. He has given multiple interviews and has got rejected at every one of them. Over a period of time every next opportunity he gets for an interview he ends up expecting the HR person rejecting him. His negative outlook is pulling him back from giving his 100% at his interview and probably proves he is not so serious about the opportunity.

Have you experienced such a situation
where your negativity has overpowered your
ability to perform your best?

Stop resisting change or growth and start looking at each opportunity with an optimistic eyeglass that can transform your life. Don't shy away. Be open to get rid of the old and accept the new. Avoid trying to control every aspect of your life. Most of the things that form our lives are beyond our reach. Focus on what you can control and let go of what you cannot. This keeps the power to change your life in your hands.

People don't resist change. They resist being changed.
– Peter Senge

What matters?

Ask yourself,

Am I Happy?
Am I where I want to be in life?
Am I using my abilities to the best of my capacity?

Reflect on where you are at this point in your life, are you where you want to be? Are your life's values and priorities aligned? In the hustle and bustle of daily life, we easily tend to forget what is important and what we need to focus on to progress in our lives. The mundane takes over and the vital get side-lined. Keep a keen eye on what matters. If its financial independence then do you control your finances or does your monthly income control your life? If it's a business deal are you steering the conversation in the right direction to close the deal, or have you let the deal pivot directionless?

Pay attention to what matters, prioritize your goals, even if it means starting each day purposefully to achieve something.

Don't let life guide you; it is high time you guide your life.

Every opportunity comes with a learning curve that leads you to success.

— Rajesh Yadav

All of these life lessons boil down to one very important question,

YOU are responsible for the direction your life takes, the values that you imbibe and the mission or goals you have set for yourself. YOU are responsible for every action, reaction and its consequences.

When you take control of your life you become the captain and navigator on your 'ship of life'.

You do not seek permission from others, but you accept guidance.

You do not seek validation from others but are open to critical feedback.

You become aware of your actions and their repercussions.

You learn to accept your faults and failures and decipher your strengths and capabilities.

You nurture the relationships you build and learn to be mindful of others.

You begin to accept the faults and failures in your close relationships and learn to harness their strengths and abilities.

You become the decision maker and avoid following the herd.

You take charge of your life and begin steering it to achieve your goals and ambitions.

You fail, you learn, you return.

Take control of your life, and you will be less susceptible to unhappiness and more open to success.

— Rajesh Yadav

❑

Thought-Provoking Questions To Ponder On

- What are you determined to accomplish in your life?
- What is it you are passionate about?
- Where does your passion intersect with your capabilities?
- How many times have you missed opportunities to upskill yourself?
- Have you let go of these opportunities because you truly lack the time?
- Or was it your comfort zone that you were protecting?
- Have you experienced such a situation where your negativity has overpowered your ability to perform your best?
- Are you Happy?
- Are you where you want to be in life?
- Are you using your abilities to the best of your capacity?